# IN THE VALLEY OF THE HEADLESS MEN

*a novella by* L.P. Hernandez

**CEMETERY GATES**
MEDIA

*In the Valley of the Headless Men*
Published by Cemetery Gates Media
Binghamton, New York

Copyright © 2024
By L.P. Hernandez

All rights reserved. Without limiting the rights under the copyright reserved above, no part of this publication may be reproduced, stored in, or introduced into a retrieval system, or transmitted in any form or by any means (electronic, mechanical, photocopying, recording, or otherwise) without prior written permission.

ISBN: 9798869581372

For more information about this book and other Cemetery Gates Media publications, visit us at:

cemeterygatesmedia.com
twitter.com/cemeterygatesm
instagram.com/cemeterygatesm


Front cover illustration by Brett Bullion

Cover wrap formatting by Geoff Parrell with Numb Phase Design

**Content Warning**: Stillbirth, loss of parent, child abuse, drug use, body horror.

*Dedicated to my brother, Jimmie, who always protected me.*

# CHAPTER ONE

The red silk scarf my mother wore countless times in life felt like mummy wrappings between my fingers. This could not have been hers. She never wore it. Her death made every memory of her feel like a lie, like a misremembered scene from a movie. The air in her room smelled different, the essence of her coming and going, of her favorite eucalyptus shampoo purged by a breeze through an open window. The lace curtains fluttered. They were not her curtains. They never were.

There is a certain age where *unexpected*, as a preface, is abandoned in favor of *unfortunate*. A seventy-year-old woman does not die unexpectedly, even one in good health. And so, it was unfortunate she died a day after our final conversation about the weather. Nothing more than the weather.

"You okay, Bro?" Oscar said.

I shook my head, clearing cobwebs. *Bro* was his term for me, not mine for him. It felt representative of a bond we never developed.

"Yeah, just thinking about the last time we spoke."

Oscar entered the room, hands in the pockets of his jeans. The collar of his dress shirt was warped from having been tugged in one or two minute intervals. Hence the hands in pockets.

"Oh? About what?"

He joined me at the foot of Mom's bed, pinching the silk scarf and rolling it between his fingers. The *half* aspect of our half-brother relationship was evident when in close proximity. He was as wide as a refrigerator with arms like sausage links. I have never been accused of being tall but could see the full crown of his head. More silver than I remembered. Probably more silver in mine too.

"She hoped it would rain. Said it was getting hot out and she hoped the rain would help her sunflowers grow."

In tandem, our gazes fell to the window, to the untamed garden beyond it. Who would care for it now? I lived an hour away and Oscar was twice as far. My eyes twitched, nostrils flaring. Part of me was not present during her service. The words and music were like a television playing in an adjoining room. The shape of it was lost, the meaning accompanying the shape. I shook so many hands, had so many conversations I could never have recalled. The ceremony did not devastate me in the way the sight of Mom's garden did in that moment.

Seventy years on this earth had earned her a few hundred square feet of it. And she did what she could to make it beautiful, to pull life from the greedy soil. Without care, without intervention the garden would yield to the spiteful summer sun. Her efforts would be petals on the wind. What was green would be brown, indistinguishable from the dirt from which it came.

"Better than mine I guess," Oscar said, clapping my left shoulder. "Last time Mom called was to get the password for Netflix."

I scoffed, "At least you helped her with something."

We stood together at the foot of Mom's bed until the silence felt like an implication. Words did not come easily between us. It was always an awkward dance, two partners with a different rhythm in their ears. Time had not affected the melody. We were forever hearing different songs.

"I'll, uh, start in the office. Is there anything you're looking for?" Oscar said.

Our goal at Mom's house was to claim any sentimental item we did not want appraised for the estate sale. At the time I could not even picture the office. It was not a room I often visited when staying there.

"Use your best judgment. If you find anything interesting or anything of mine let me know. I'll look around here and do the same."

Oscar left, whistling. I hated when he did that. It was never a song I recognized. Just some random tune.

I began with her nightstand. When I pulled the drawer open I caught a gust of her, but it was drawn out the window. The diary I bought her two, maybe ten Christmases ago stood out amid cough drops and old credit cards she refused to throw away. Mom was convinced her identity would be stolen even if she cut the cards into confetti and threw them away in separate garbage bags. I plucked the diary out of the drawer and sat on the bed. This was not why I was here. To invade my mother's private thoughts. I glanced at the door. Oscar was still whistling, and it was the first time I could remember being grateful for it.

I opened the front cover and found her name along with a date. Apparently, it was five Christmases ago.

"Sorry Mom," I whispered, and turned the page.

It was blank. I turned another. Blank. She had never used it. I don't know why I thought she would.

***

Half an hour passed with nothing more interesting than the unused diary. There were a few framed pictures on her dressers. Oscar, me, and Mom modeling the worst fashion of the 80s and 90s. Billowy shirts and streetwise cartoon characters. No pictures of our fathers, though I would not have expected them. Oscar's father's name was uttered so infrequently growing up I would have needed several guesses to recall it. My father was not a forbidden topic so much as a forgotten one.

I placed the pictures on the bed planning to give Oscar the first choice. Being a big brother came with perks. I was surprised visiting Oscar's place after not having done so for several years. Surprised to find myself featured so prominently on his walls and bookshelves. For much of his adult life, Oscar had no home. Where had he stored the pictures then? When he was living in hotels and alleys? Maybe Mom gave them to him when he got clean.

The whistling had stopped. I cocked my head, angled my ear to the door.

"Oscar?"

He did not reply, and I stepped into the hall wondering if he might have left while I was daydreaming.

"Uh, Bro, I got something you're gonna wanna see."

High school versions of me appraised my slow walk down the hallway. The office door was the only one ajar, a rhomboid of sunlight stretching across the floor.

"What is it?" I asked as I entered the room.

Oscar sat on a stool in front of Mom's roll top desk. He had given up tugging his collar in favor of unbuttoning the shirt. A patchwork of blurry tattoos spread across his arms and chest. Spanish words he might not have known the definition of. Pictures and symbols drawn by an unsteady hand, maybe Oscar himself. They were faded, like the life he'd left behind.

"What is it?" I said again.

He fanned out the envelopes I hadn't noticed he was holding.

"They're from your dad."

\*\*\*

We migrated to the dining room. The sunflowers Mom had picked only a few days ago drooped in their vase, the water no longer sustaining them. This was not the home we grew up in. There were many *houses* growing up. Many apartments. I don't know if any place ever felt like *home*. But Mom did. Wherever Mom went, that was home.

"It's still weird, man."

"What's that?" Oscar said, sitting up in his chair.

"You drinking water."

His laugh must have come from his father, because it was unique in our family. A belly shake with a clicking sound at the back of his throat.

"How do you know it's not gin?"

I joined him in laughter, "You'd have both shirts off if it was."

More belly shaking and clicking.

"That's true, Bro. I wouldn't remember tomorrow, though. I go hard on gin. I mean, I did."

He tapped his knuckles on the table next to the stack of envelopes. The thought of my father unlocked many closed doors in my mind. I sensed them, the faint light spilling through, mostly darkness. These were memories I kept out of the sun, hoping they would fade like Oscar's tattoos. Maybe in darkness they would become unrecognizable, only surfacing in dreams, shapes without meaning.

"It's okay if you don't wanna open them here," Oscar said.

I had already decided I wouldn't. Our fathers were what kept us from being *real* brothers. Real. That word a special sort of ammunition. As kids we hurled it in anger so frequently it lost meaning. Those projectiles built a wall, and its structure was secure decades later. My father was a ghost. Oscar's father was a demon. Different specters, but we were both haunted.

"I'll probably open them at home. Not sure when. My mind's so full of Mom, I wasn't really prepared to think about him."

"Understood, Bro. I hope it's good. Whatever's in those letters I hope it's good. Don't judge Mom for not giving them to you. I- I can't speak to her reasoning on that, and, I guess she took it with her. So, if it's good or bad, just know she kept it from you for the right reasons. I remember those weekends when your dad was supposed to visit. You'd stay by the window starting Friday afternoon, peeking through the blinds. You wouldn't leave until Sunday evening. I saw it too many times, Bro. He didn't deserve you as a son."

Our eyes met. His a slightly lighter shade of brown. Mom came through in his cheekbones, the shape of his brow. She came through me in the same way. Oscar was now my closest relative. We shared the most blood. We shared her blood.

"I...thank you. You know I feel the same about you and your dad. Guess that goes without saying."

He smiled, a finger tracing the scar below his eye. His father's doing.

"We didn't pick our dads. I'm not even sure Mom did. They were bad guys who took advantage of a young woman with too much trust."

My dad's handwriting was familiar in a way that filled my stomach with hailstones, rough and cold. It was my handwriting. Not every letter, but most of them. He departed my life decades ago, but part of him remained and it always would. A ghost guiding my hand, shaping my letters to look like his.

\*\*\*

I drove for miles in silence, the setting sun an unreachable target before me. How many more times would I make this trip, I wondered. After the estate sale and the house was sold, what reason would I have to come back? All those hours Mom spent watering flowers, trimming unhealthy stalks, rejoicing at the appearance of a single pepper…None of it mattered. The flowers were dying. Without tending, the peppers would not survive a month of Texas summer.

The envelopes felt like a hornet's nest in the passenger seat. Thankfully, the route home was so familiar I could drive on autopilot, because I had one eye off the road. I knew the contents of those envelopes would change me. It would reveal more about both my father and mother. Perhaps there was an excuse for every missed weekend visit, for every forgotten birthday. Maybe to Mom the excuses weren't good enough.

This moment, serenaded by the drone of asphalt under tires, was unrecoverable. I would never have the luxury of not knowing. I would never have this peace. If I opened one letter, I would open the others. They would change me. I could not imagine feeling better about either of my parents after reading them.

Without thinking about it, I pressed the button to roll down the passenger window. The wind rushed in, and the envelopes quivered in the seat. I did not have to do this. I could let the wind turn the letters into tumbleweeds. Mom would forever rest upon her pedestal, and Dad would be invisible in its shadow.

The letters lifted, halfway to standing upright. I smacked them to the seat and lowered the window.

\*\*\*

I would read the first and no more. I promised it on my dead mother. Having spoken those words aloud, I did not open the first letter. I held it, felt the caterpillar fuzz of the worn edges. It was dated two weeks after my birthday, meaning he likely realized it after the fact.

I sat in the living room, tumbler half-filled with whiskey in one hand, the envelope in the other. Why had Mom not given it to me? Why did she take that choice away?

I pried at the corner, scraped the tape that sealed it shut for the past thirty years. As I did I caught sight of my wedding ring. I wore it the last time I saw her hoping it would convey something my words did not. The tan line on her ring finger was no longer distinguishable. She had given me all of our pictures.

"Are you sure?" I asked.

She nodded, arms crossed, eyes narrowed as if struggling to make sense of something across the room.

"You could take a few..." I offered.

She licked her teeth before speaking, "Why would I want to do that?"

Because we had ten years together. Because they weren't all bad. Because I might not have been your life partner, in the end, but our time mattered. I took them but did not hang them. They were in a box in the garage. Compartmentalized.

I slid the ring off my finger and placed it on the coffee table. I massaged the indentation in the skin until it disappeared.

*To endings.*

I sipped the whiskey and ripped open the first letter.

\*\*\*

Oscar cleared his throat, but his words were jagged, "What's up, Bro?"

"You sleeping? I can call tomorrow."

He laughed, "It *is* tomorrow, Bro. What's up?"

The white noise of the box fan faded as he walked out of his bedroom.

"Sorry if I woke Isa. The baby's not in the room with you is she?"

"Nah, you're good, Bro. She's not even a baby anymore, technically. A pre-toddler or some shit? I don't know where they come up with these terms. And Isa sleeps with earplugs. Don't worry about her. I'm guessing you opened them?"

What is the penalty for breaking a promise on your dead mother? She could not be *more* dead.

"I didn't mean to. I thought maybe it...the first one...would be my dad apologizing for forgetting my birthday. He didn't. I don't think he remembered it was my birthday. After the first one I had to read the second, because that couldn't be it. It was so...it didn't change anything."

"Damn. I'm sorry."

"Maybe the next one would tell me something. Maybe he would wonder why I didn't respond. He didn't. At least he remembered he forgot my birthday, but the letter was about him. So was the next one. All of 'em. He'd say things like...like when I visit we could go see this or that. But there was no plan. It was almost like a journal, like he was writing notes to himself. I kept opening them, kept reading but they were all the same. The last few were shorter. He met a woman who had kids. Said I would get along with them. He was retiring from the Air Force and settling down in Oregon."

Ice clinked in a cup on Oscar's end, and he whispered, "Oh, shit. Sorry. Didn't realize that would be so loud. So, he started a new family in Oregon? That it?"

The final letter was different. The tone, even the handwriting. I could sense his excitement in the shaky letters, as if he wrote it while running to the post office. Having learned very little about my father in the previous letters, it was also bewildering.

"No. There was one letter that I wanted to talk to you about."

"Oh? Did he ask about me?"

I brought the tumbler to my lips, but the whiskey was gone. Half a bottle in one night. Damn.

"No. No he didn't. He wrote about a trip he was taking. To Canada. Some park way up north. I looked it up after I read the letter. It's really there. Not that I thought he was lying about it. Just, it was so strange. So different from every other letter."

Oscar yawned, "Yeah, that's weird, Bro."

I was failing at conveying how strange, how distinct the letter was from the others. It was dated two years after the second most recent. There was this voice coming through, this vitality. Passion. That's what it was.

"It felt like he was communicating to me, Oscar. I know it's a letter and that's the point. But none of the others felt like that."

He groaned as he sat, the faint sound of ice tinkling in his glass before he spoke, "Not sure I follow."

"He said he was going there to find himself."

"I hope it worked out for him."

"If you're ever feeling lost, Joseph, you should too."

"Huh?"

"That's the last line in the letter. That's the last thing my father ever wrote to me."

"Damn. Well, now you've got me interested. Gonna be tough to fall asleep. What's the name of the park?"

Before calling Oscar, I had spent an hour researching. It was beautiful, remote. I could not picture my father there, but something had drawn him to it.

"It has two names. The official name is Nahanni National Park."

"Gonna need help spelling that. What's the other?"

"The Valley of the Headless Men."

# CHAPTER TWO

Gillian re-entered my life a few months ago. She picked up on the social media cues, my ex-wife's profile picture changing from us to her shimmering legs on a beach. More girl's nights. More quotes about letting go and becoming who you were meant to be. But she was courteous. She checked in with a simple, *Everything okay?* I did not reply. A month passed before she tried again. Another month and I finally answered.

J: *I think 'okay' covers the spectrum of what I'm feeling.*
G: *Oh? Care to share?*
J: *It's not great. Not awful. Just okay.*
G: *It's okay to not be okay. That's what my therapist says.*
J: *Okay is the sweet spot for me. Good is aspirational.*
G: *I'm here if you need a friend* 😊

I did not ask if friendship was the extent of what she sought. We tried it before, too many times. A few weeks or months into the experiment she would ask the question.

*What do you think he would have been like?*
Or
*What would he be doing now?*

She said he had my eyes, but I never saw them open. Maybe she imagined it. He was beautiful. Perfect. Except for the still organ in the center of his chest. I did not carry him inside of me. Our lives were not intertwined in that way. I watched her belly grow, felt his kicks and punches toward the end. All contained, hidden within her. Gillian knew him as a living thing. When I touched his face with the back of my hand his cheeks were already cool.

As a couple, we did not survive the death of our son. Gillian had a new partner, not a romantic one. She woke to a nightstand picture of him in utero, thumb to lips as if rehearsing for her. She carried the socks he wore, for two hours, in her pocket like a worry stone. We planned to name him in the delivery room, but that did not happen. A month after the stillbirth, Gillian was still researching names. What do you name a child who knew only darkness?

I did not lead her on intentionally, though our friendship experiments were sometimes physical. Before Cheryl I was lonely, and Gillian loved me like no one else had. Not to suggest it was better, just unequaled.

*Do you want to try again?*

The question encompassed so many possibilities, so many future paths. At twenty-three, I realized I didn't. Not with her. I had joined the military not out of patriotism or sense of legacy but desperation. A fresh start, but there were tears in her eyes. Her question only meant one thing.

I spoke with Oscar until my cell phone was as hot as a sun-warmed brick, the battery nearing its limit. Then I passed out on the couch. The whiskey flavored my dreams with menace, the images of Nahanni combined with the idea my father was still there somehow. Like a cryptid in the periphery, never in focus. It was dream logic, not rooted in truth, but when I woke mid-morning, tongue as dry as a summer sidewalk, it felt like a message.

I was to head back to Mom's house. By the time I woke Oscar was probably already on the road. I subdued the hangover in its tremor state with water and breakfast burritos, and the dreamscape slipped from my memories like water seeping through the seams of my fingers.

*Thinking about you, J. You've been through a lot this year. Remember what I said about being okay.*

Twenty years and she had never married, never had a serious relationship from what I saw online. A not small part of my ego was convinced she was waiting for me. As my marriage unraveled, I depended on the idea that someone thought I was worthy.

Oscar was in the front yard. Slacks dyed green from calf to hem from cut grass, cowboy boots, and no shirt. His brown skin glistened like a chicken on a spit. As I parked, he cut the mower's engine and pulled a handkerchief from his pocket. He wiped the sweat from his brow and chest, then tucked the bandana in his pocket.

"I couldn't watch it go to shit, Bro. While it's still hers, you know?"

Yes, I knew. Had he not been so sweaty I would have hugged him. Instead, I clapped his shoulder.

"Now it's just us," I said, the nearest to a sentimental observation I can recall sharing with him.

"Do you think," he began, then paused to wipe newly formed sweat on his brow. "We can make up for lost time? I know we haven't been involved in each other's lives much. I was dealing with my shit, and you went off to explore the world. But now we're both here. Maybe it's time."

"Time?"

There was more structure to the words he danced around, an idea I sensed the edges of. He nodded to the door and led the way. Inside, we returned to our seats at Mom's dining room table.

Of all the rooms in the house, the kitchen had been the busiest. *Had* been. It was quiet now, just the refrigerator humming. This is the part of dying no one talks about. The stuff. The half-filled container of flour, the olive oil. Mom would have made magic with it. But it wasn't worth taking, not really. None of it was. I pictured Mom in the supermarket, buying the flour with plans for bread or cookies. She came to baking later in life, a hobby she did not have time for when we were kids. Now, it was garbage.

"Feels kinda strange drinking the last of Mom's lemonade," he said.

"It does."

He downed half the glass as if it was gin and he needed the courage. Then we wiped his mouth and lightly pounded the table.

"So! We're going."

"Going?"

"The Valley of the Headless Men. You can't drop that on someone and expect them to just go to sleep. I stayed up 'til four reading about it. You got me hooked, man. You want to go. I know you do. And your big brother's going with you."

My heart felt like a pile of feathers. The air in my lungs was weightless. Did I want to go? It was the last thing my father ever wrote to me. I had looked his name up, wondering if the reason for it being the final missive was because the Valley had claimed him. There were a few hits after the date of the letter, but nothing for the past fifteen years. Perhaps he'd gone back. Perhaps he'd never returned.

"You're assuming a lot."

"Am I?" Oscar said, his father's laugh threatening in his chest. "We may not be best friends, Bro, but I know you. I know the books you used to read. I still remember how excited you got when they sent those flyers home. The book ones? Mom would send you with a ten dollar check and you'd stretch that thing to the moon. Make deals to get more books. You were never satisfied. Readin' the last page of one and you'd have your thumb in another."

I smiled at the memory.

"And what do my childhood books have to do with going to a haunted national park in Canada?"

He finished his lemonade before responding. The pitcher was between us. Oscar nodded at it, and I shrugged.

He spoke as he poured, "You're curious. About everything. But this is different. Ernie cast a long shadow, Bro. I saw it plenty when we were kids. Like I said, we haven't been close since we grew up. I had my stuff, you know. Made my mistakes. Hey, one of us had to make Ma proud."

"She was proud of you, Oscar. She hurt for you, but she was never not proud. Despite everything you've been through you're still a good person. I can't say the same for myself."

Oscar's fingers danced over his stubble. He cast an unfocused gaze at the refrigerator.

"You're trying to throw me off, and I'm not gonna let you. Look, you just got out of the military. Your marriage is, well, it is what it is. Or was. Sorry. We spent the first half of our lives as strangers. Why not? Why not go have an adventure with your brother? I was gonna suggest Vegas, but this is better. Too many lights there. Too much noise. There's a lot I don't know about you little bro. Probably heard about me through Mom over the years, but that's not the same as having a conversation."

Oscar retrieved the lemonade. It was the last of it. The last of Mom's lemonade. He cocked an eyebrow and I shrugged again. It was easy to do the little things with Oscar. Easy to make it seem like I was trying. Oscar poured the glass to just over half full but didn't drink. He picked it up and stared, maybe coming to the same realization as me. The threads connecting us to this woman, the most important person in either of our lives, were snapping. Although maybe that's too severe a visual. They were unraveling. Our memories of her would lose color every day, like a painting forgotten in the sun. Eventually, the only threads left would be us; me and Oscar.

My big brother was just past middle age. His beard was more silver than black now. The scar his father gave him blended with the wrinkles around his eye. I could not have said, in that moment, what his favorite movie was. I did not know his passions or his dreams for the future. There was a reason for it, a reason like a seed in my mind. I never gave it sun, refused to let the roots grow.

"They still allow you to travel outside the country?"

He laughed, "Bro, it was jail. Not prison. That stuff's not in my record anyway. Remember I went to Cabo? We think that's where we got pregnant."

"Oh, I didn't realize it happened to both of you."

He drank until there was just a sip left, then placed the glass on the table.

"It felt like it. Had me runnin' out at midnight for snacks like some sitcom dad. Put on twenty pounds 'cause she never wanted them by the time I got back."

"Not our dads."

"That's true. Least mine finally died so I could piss on his grave."

I sat up, "Did you?"

Oscar winked, "I'll tell you about it when we're there."

\*\*\*

We worked as a team for the rest of the day. There was a familiarity to his presence, the rhythm of his speech. But it was also different. The decades since the last time we shared a roof had changed him. Probably changed me in his eyes. I was barely a teen when Oscar left home, a four-year stint in the Army precipitating fifteen years of struggling.

"Gotta go be a dad," Oscar announced after checking his cell.

"Back tomorrow?"

He shrugged, "Probably not. Can't take too much time off work. I don't have a retirement check unlike some people. I'll try to come back, though, before the estate sale."

I realized I was going to miss him. Maybe it was that seed inside of me, the one I kept in the dark. I felt it shivering.

Before I knew I would speak the words they hung in the air between us.

"Let's do it."

"The trip? Yeah?"

"I'm retired. Got enough stashed for a couple years if I need. Let's do it. Maybe my dad died up there and we can piss on his grave together."

I drove home feeling better about things. I was not thankful to have lost Mom, but thankful something good would come from it. It would have made her happy to see her two boys becoming friends.

I returned the missed call from Gillian as I drove.

"Hey stranger," she said.

"Hey."

"Busy day at your Mom's?"

"Yeah. Got through a lot of it. It's weird. The whole thing is weird, but this part especially. You're sorting kitchen stuff and next thing you know you're in a puddle of tears because of a pair of oven mitts. You know, the memories."

"She was wonderful, Joseph. I'm sorry you're hurting. She always had a special place with me," Gillian said, and after a pause added. "How's Oscar?"

"Oh, doing okay. Same for him, though. We talked most of the day, but sometimes he'd go quiet and I'd look over to see him holding a picture or a cookbook and crying."

"Oh, poor Oscar. I only met him a few times, but he always seemed like a big softy to me."

"He is. Having the little one is ramping that up. He's so excited to be a dad. Like it's what he was meant to do."

I swallowed, squeezed the steering wheel until the blood drained from my knuckles. I imagined Gillian's thoughts listening to me speak of fatherhood. Was she substituting me in his place? Instead of Oscar chasing around his daughter it was me with our son?

"I'm so happy for him. I know things weren't easy."

"Yeah. Yeah they weren't. Always felt guilty about that," I said. Maybe enough time had passed. Maybe we could be friends without the impossible detours. "Something unexpected came out of it. I mean, I had no idea this place even existed."

"Place?"

"Oh, I didn't tell you about the letters. Oscar found them in Mom's office. They were from my dad. Nothing really special. Just the same old, self-congratulatory stuff. Except for one. The last letter talked about this…national park up in Canada. Way up there. Dad was taking a trip for some reason he didn't really explain. It was a shorter letter. Anyway, this place has a weird history, although *history* might not be the most accurate word for it. There's rumors of giants, of supposedly extinct mammals like mammoths. Oh, and headless men. A lot of them. Enough so that its alternate name is The Valley of the Headless Men. Just…strange."

I did not realize how excited I was until then.

"Strange is a good word for it. So, what about the place?"

"We're going. Still working out the details of when. Might have to wait until next year, but we're going. Have an adventure, you know?"

"Hmmm..." Gillian said, and for a moment the only sound was the thrum of my tires over asphalt. "Doesn't seem like you."

I chuckled at that. Our banter felt normal, as if the time and circumstances between us were illusions.

"Why doesn't it?"

"Please, Joe, you're not the *on a whim* type. You used to look up the best parking spots before we went out to eat."

"Well, it saves time. Parking is the worst part of going out."

"True. And, I do it now, too. Don't let it go to your head."

I parked in my driveway. Maybe if I had called her five minutes later, had ended the call five minutes sooner things would have been different.

"I'll be sure to check parking for the Valley before I go."

"Sounds good, Joe. So when are we going?"

\*\*\*

"Are you sure, Bro?"

"It's not really my choice. I can't stop her from buying a ticket."

"I was hoping we'd be there alone, you know?"

I wiped sweat onto the back of my arm, then kneed the box of military mementos onto a shelf in the garage. A whole life, a whole identity fit into that box.

"Yeah, I know. But like I said, can't stop her from buying a ticket. She's part of my life. Always has been."

Oscar sent puffs of static through the phone. It was not my idea, but I did not push back when she suggested it. A buffer might be useful. Someone to ease the tension...not that I anticipated any.

"You there Oscar?"

...
...

"Hello?"

*Son,*

*Sorry I missed my weekend with you, bud. Usually, your mom is good about reminding me, but I guess she forgot this time. I'll make it up to you soon. You can stay up late and rent movies. How does that sound?*

*Speaking of your mom. Does she talk about me? It's tough not being there to defend myself. I can only imagine the things she says. Probably makes me out to be a monster. But I only wanted the best for you and Oscar. He isn't my blood, but I treated him the same. That wasn't always easy to do. Oscar can be difficult. Your mom and I had different ideas on how to handle that.*

*Anyway, I miss being at home. Going from a house to an apartment, not having your mother around to cook isn't easy. But I've got a couple dates lined up this week and next. They're not your mother, but hopefully they'll like to cook. Oh, you don't mind if your next weekend is just one day, do you?*

*Take care of your mom. Will see you soon.*

*Love,*
*Dad*

# CHAPTER THREE

I gave Oscar my trust and money, unsure of how we would reach Nahanni but believing it was his puzzle to solve. Like with all problems since he was a child, Oscar's solution was to barrel through them as if they did not exist. After multiple flights on progressively smaller planes, we arrived at Fort Simpson off-season. I did not know it was off-season when we landed. My research into Nahanni was not logistical in nature. No, I read about the stories of giants, hidden caverns and thermal springs supporting tropical vegetation. I read about monsters and headless men.

I was too tired from the journey to notice the confusion of the hotel staff, who were unaccustomed to the sight of tourists in early June. There was no masking our intentions. We had the gear and the self-assuredness of Americans in a foreign environment. Perhaps that confidence kept well intentioned locals heading to the hotel's bar from speaking up. There were no scheduled flights to Nahanni for another month. Our return flight to the states was in less than ten days. I did not know it then, barely standing upright in the lobby and unsure of what day it was.

My brother and I shared a room and Gillian had the one neighboring. We showered and changed clothes but did not unpack as we were supposed to depart tomorrow. *Supposed to* was a term I did not realize had not been fleshed out.

"What time do we need to be up?" I asked.

Oscar was in the bathroom refreshing the gel in his hair.

"Oh, uh, pretty early."

More than his words, I picked up on the way he spoke them, the hint of surprise at being asked.

"Oscar…"

"What's up, Bro?" he said, angling his body so I could not see his face in the bathroom mirror.

"What time do we leave?"

Another delay. Water running. He began to cough and spit into the sink to buy himself time. He emerged half a minute later, hair glistening but unkempt, blotting his face with a towel.

"I need to meet a guy."

My face likely showed the confusion I felt. I was already a few grand down with flight costs and gear. The money was recoverable, but not knowing my immediate future turned my stomach into a clenched fist.

"What do you mean *meet a guy*?"

Oscar rubbed his hands together, eyes shifting to the carpet.

"So, we're actually here early. The tourist season doesn't start until later in the month."

Instead of peppering him with the questions building steam in my lungs I left space for him to speak.

"I didn't want to do the tourist thing with you, Bro. I wanted it to be us. You and me."

"Gillian?"

He shrugged, "That was your call. I couldn't change that. But this part I can. I don't want to go sightseeing, man. There are places a lot closer to home for that. Once I found out about this place, I felt called to it. Like we're supposed to be here."

"Oscar, I'm not upset. I just don't understand. How are we going to get there?"

His smile returned, his father's laugh rumbling in the back of his throat, "I told you. I need to meet a guy."

\*\*\*

Oscar returned to the bathroom and, after fixing his hair, slid out the door before I could harass him further. I sat on the bed unsure of what to do next. Despite the rattling heater doing its best the room was like the freezer section of the grocery store. The tips of my ears throbbed, and my nose felt like it had been dipped in ice cream. It was late spring back home, warm, the bluebonnets turning hills into ocean waves.

The divorce was done, and I would be rejoining the workforce upon my return. Gillian and I stayed in touch in the months since my mother passed and Oscar proposed this wild idea. We were friends, genuinely, and it felt good.

With so much to look forward to, this trip felt like the first chapter of the second half of my life story. It meant a lot to Oscar, and we were closer now than when we last shared a bunk bed. Based on his cryptic words, it was quite possible the trip would not happen, though. Meaning I spent several thousand dollars on a vacation to a northern Canadian village with fewer residents than my childhood middle school.

"Anyone home?" Gillian called, accompanying the question with a knock.

The springs sang as I hopped off the bed. I opened the door, and she took half a step in before retreating into the hall.

"Oh, God, it's like a walk-in!" she said. "Come to my room. It's cozy."

When we were together, I found the word *beautiful* difficult to speak. Not because she wasn't. Because I knew she needed to hear it. The word was like a high diver on the tip of my tongue, scooting to the edge of the platform, toes curled and trembling. Her hair was wet from the shower, thin sweater clinging and spotted with water droplets. I knew what was beneath, had helped her undress many times, but my pulse still quickened. My blood felt like static in my veins.

"What?" she asked, smiling but allowing the confusion to settle across her brow.

I had the strangest urge to tuck a stray, auburn lock behind her ear, but my hand was well trained. Doing so would mean something. That the towering wall between friendship and what lay beyond was only sand. The distance between us was self-imposed. I once thought of it like the lion and the antelope who have decided to become friends. The instinct is there, the familiarity of the hunt. How easy it would be to slip into old habits, to give in.

"It's so damn cold," I said, unable to hold her gaze.

Did she sense it? It would only take a word or a gesture. But I couldn't do that to her again. Though never with malice, I had broken her too many times.

"Come on over. It's not warm, but it's warmer than here," she said.

I followed behind. Her room was a duplicate of mine, down to the framed photographs of what I assumed was Nahanni. It smelled better. Her scent. Some sweet buttery lotion that made my mouth water.

"Where's Oscar?"

"That's potentially a bad news, bad news situation."

She sat on the bed and patted the space next to her.

"What do you mean?"

The comforter was as rigid as an Autumn leaf. I left a foot between us.

"I thought the flight into Nahanni was a done deal."

"It's not?"

I shrugged, "That's an Oscar question. He's sorting it out now, but I have no idea what that entails."

"Oh," she said. "Well, I hope there are no hiccups. I really wanna go."

"I blame myself. Oscar's come a long way as a person, but he's still a *figure it out* kinda guy."

"What if it doesn't get sorted? Is there any other way to get there?"

"If the wind is blowing the right direction maybe kite surfing?"

She gave me a little shove, "Oh, right. That's what northern Canada is known for. Actually, I saw a stack of board games in the lobby."

"And there's a bar."

"It'll be like old times," she said, then leaned over to rest her head on my shoulder. I stiffened and tilted away from her. She must have felt it.

"Oh, relax Joseph. After everything we've been through you should feel more at ease around me than anyone on earth. I've seen you cry into a toilet. You gave me strep throat-"

"You had it first! You were just asymptomatic!"

Another playful shove.

"Maybe when we die and we get to watch the movie of our lives we'll know. We'll finally know who the bastard was that gave the other strep throat."

"If it was you I'm gonna find you in hell."

"That's my Joseph," she said, and patted the top of my thigh. Her hand stayed and I didn't move it.

"Cheryl hated you, you know."

"Feeling was mutual."

I laughed, "Why's that?"

She sandwiched my hand between hers.

"You're a great guy. You know that…"

"Agree to disagree on that."

"Fine. You're a great guy and a contrarian. You're not just a great guy, Joe. You're a good person. That's rarer than you might think. There were other guys after you. A couple of long-term ones. I learned from them you can be a great guy and not a good person. It's actually pretty easy. You say the right things. You open doors and remember anniversaries. That's not *goodness*. That's checking boxes. And you know what they all had in common? They *told* people they were good guys."

"Really?"

"Really. Didn't matter the type. Sweater vest or football jersey. Ugh, it was so exhausting. Men wanting to be thanked."

What did she see that I didn't?

We heard Oscar's approach well before his face appeared between the door and the frame. He was sweating, somehow, cheeks puffing as his lungs struggled to keep up with the demands of his body.

"I told you," he gasped.

"Told me?"

"I needed to meet a guy. And I did. Pilot Bob. A couple folks on the message boards mentioned him."

"Pilot Bob?" I said.

"Message boards?" Gillian said.

Oscar entered the room and perched his hands on his hips, "He's a good guy. Used to fly for one of the local companies but…"

"But?" Gillian prodded.

"He'll tell you. It's actually a good thing because now he can fly out of season. Has his own plane and everything. There's rules about when you can visit the Valley, so he lands just outside of it. Then it's on us."

"And he'll take us?" I said.

Oscar wiggled a hand in the air, "I'm close. He's buzzed right now, tryin' to nudge him over the edge. You guys should come down. He wants to meet you and he's got lots of stories!"

"Buzzed…" I mumbled.

Gillian patted my thigh again and stood, "You wanted an adventure!"

***

Beer was flowing, but Pilot Bob went for the stiffer stuff. He crowed when Oscar returned, wrapping my brother in a bear hug as if he hadn't departed two minutes prior. The bar area was balmy compared to my room, but my body was still shedding the chill and I could not stop my teeth from chattering. Bob moved Oscar aside and hugged me, then Gillian with the same vigor.

"My Americans!" he said, kissing Oscar on the cheek.

He looked like a skinny Santa Claus, cheeks nearly purple from snow burn, eyes like glaciers, which was fitting. His beard hair was wispy like the Great Pyrenees Gillian and I adopted early in our relationship. She kept the dog after we separated, and on subsequent visits he treated me like a stranger.

"Don't get many Americans up here?" Gillian asked.

Pilot Bob either did not hear or ignored the question, "We must drink!"

There was a hint of an accent blurred by the liquor. Scandinavian? I did not know my Canadian accents well. He could have been local. At his invitation, and with my brother refreshing the stack of bills on the bar, we did drink. Canadian whisky precipitating a road trip through Kentucky and Tennessee. Within an hour, both Bobs, as I was seeing two of them, invited us to sit at a table. My belly was hot with liquor. Dwight Yoakam twanged over speakers that hissed like bacon on a skillet. I felt good. Relaxed.

"You fly there often? The Valley?" I asked.

"Oh, yah, for sure. Been goin' since the 70s I imagine. First as a tourist like you lot. Got my license in, oh, '72 or so."

"So, you're not from here? You came as a tourist?"

Pilot Bob scratched his chin, beard hairs waving.

"Oh, yah. Was just passin' through to tell truth. Hadn't ever heard of the Valley before. Was in Yellowknife just kinda bummin' around. Found that book you lot mighta read, eh? About the headless fellas. Hitched over here and stayed in this very building. Can you believe that, eh? Fifty years later and I'm still here!"

I sat taller in my chair, the whisky fog abating for a moment, "It was the Valley that kept you here?"

Pilot Bob nodded once, slowly.

"Why?"

"Look, I know why I stayed. Why are *you* here?"

The question was not directed at me, and I was surprised to find myself answering.

"To see something I've never seen before."

Pilot Bob brushed his knuckles across his cheek.

"They got trees in Texas. Don't they?"

"Not the trees. It's something else."

"What?"

"I think I won't know until I see it."

Pilot Bob's smile was an effort to prevent other emotions from surfacing.

"It called to you. Didn't it?"

Since the discovery of the letter, the Valley had been a consistent thought in my mind. A passenger so quiet I sometimes forgot he was there. I'd be tending a pot of water and find myself dreaming of mountains, of secret passageways among them. I dreamed of birds that had never before seen the face of a man, of a shadow between the trees. My father. A collection of unfamiliar shapes and colors. He called to me, but was that *his* voice? I had not heard it in so long. Maybe it was. Maybe it was Oscar.

"I'm not sure if that's something I can know, sitting here. You know why you stayed because you already experienced it. Or maybe you're hoping to. Could be it's like a hot stove, you know. I just need to touch it once."

Pilot Bob reached across the table, nearly tipping it in the process. He clamped a strong hand on my wrist.

"That's closer to the mark than you know."

***

The liquor flowed, though at the time I wasn't sure who was paying. The number of locals, most First Nations, swelled from a handful to twenty, and did not dip below that number to the point I stopped caring. News of our planned adventure spread. None attempted to talk us out of going, but they did shake our hands upon meeting as if expecting it would be for the last time. I did not know if it was appropriate to ask about the legends of the park. I feared even using that word, park, as it was a label created by a government often on the wrong side of history regarding tribal matters. Gillian, after a few shots, was not as tentative.

Oscar accompanied Pilot Bob outside for a cigarette, and their seats were claimed by an older First Nations man, his hair in a loose ponytail terminating at his waist, and a boy he introduced as his grandson.

"We know what's written. It's not a lot. What's true?" Gillian asked.

The old man smiled, "There is truth in the stories. The men? Yes, their heads were taken. Predators don't leave good meat, and they don't take souvenirs."

"What happened to them? Is it just that they went?"

"The old stories talk of giants. A brutal people. Here before us, before the Dene, some believe. Brutal, but maybe not war hungry."

"What do you mean?" I asked.

The warmth of the room, bodies creating friction in tight spaces combined with the puddle of whisky in my belly made me feel as if I was on a raft at sea. I gripped the sides of the table to keep from falling over.

"Sharp teeth are a tool. To hunt. To end a life. They are also a warning. The wolves here will show you their teeth before the attack. Not a bluff. A promise. *Take one step closer, man. Earn your place at the top.*

"It's different up there. Not a wolf showing teeth. It is Nahanni. It is the land. I have never seen a giant. No tools of theirs have been discovered. Did they exist? It only matters that our ancestors believed they existed. They did not question the evidence of their eyes, whatever was shown to them. Is it true? That is not the heart of the message. The message is the wolf's promise. Nahanni is the open mouth."

Gillian squeezed my hand. I might have been showing the fear I felt.

"Why those men? It's not an easy place to get to, but hundreds still go," I said.

Pilot Bob and Oscar returned after the question was posed. The old man smiled at Pilot Bob, but his lips thinned into a razor cut as he looked at Oscar, the collar of his shirt stained brown with spilled liquor. He struggled with moderation in every applicable sense. Hopefully, it was just the environment.

"Wolves will let hundreds of caribou pass. Thousands. Sometimes for days they wait. The caribou grow used to them, used to the smell. Even when he is still, when his gaze is turned the other direction, a wolf is always hunting."

\*\*\*

We retired after midnight. Between the travel and the alcohol, my mind felt unmoored, like a balloon floating just above my head. I hugged the mattress and swam in the still room, my thoughts just outside of my body.

It was so cold in the room. How familiar, how warm would it feel to lay beside her.

*Son,*

*Sorry I missed your birthday. I'm sending a gift in the mail. Shouldn't be too long...let me know when you get it. Hey, we'll have two birthday cakes next time. How's that?*

*Also, your mother was pretty upset I didn't tell you about the move. In the military these things happen quick. So quick you might not realize you forgot something important. I'll take the blame on this one. Honestly, I wasn't sure how to tell you, as I knew you were making plans for us this year. So, I kept putting it off, and then I ran out of time. The good news is it's only a one year tour out here. The bad news is it's more likely than not I'll be moved to D.C. after this assignment. Why don't we get excited about that? It's a big city. Lots of stuff to do when you come out for a visit.*

*Does your mother read my letters? They should really be between us. I know I haven't had a good showing lately, but I'm trying. I know she says bad things about me. Don't let her change things between us, son.*

*Wait until you see your gift!*

*Love,*
*Dad*

# CHAPTER FOUR

From the sky the terrain reminded me of the blanket issued to me during basic training, more in texture than color, as much of the landscape was covered in snow. I recalled staring at my toes, the rough, pinched fabric between my feet and chin like a series of weathered mountain ranges. When sleep didn't come, and it often didn't, I imagined a fantasy world in those mountains. Over the sound of the plane's engine, I heard the breath of fifty young men, the agitated toe-tapping of the unlucky soul tasked with guard duty. It felt like a lifetime ago, the bottom layer of a box in the garage.

Gillian sent letters, though we weren't together then. She wrote "Pictures inside!" on the envelopes because she knew the TIs would open them. Sometimes they held onto our letters as a form of blackmail, psychological games. After basic training, Gillian told me labeling the envelopes *Pictures inside* was a tip she learned online. The photos were never what the instructors hoped for. Those she sent later.

There were caribou below us, not in the thrilling numbers I expected based on nature documentaries. I assumed there were wolves as well, salivating at the memory of calves stretching their mother's bellies.

"I'm not supposed to fly you into the park. You didn't register, right? We're gonna land just outside of it. Off to the side, eh? There aren't many places to touch down. Not that *they* know about anyway. You'll have a short walk after, but don't worry, there are landmarks to guide you," Pilot Bob said, nearly yelling.

"What happens if we die in there?" Gillian asked, voice barely audible. She peeled her forehead off her small window, wide eyes suggesting she hadn't meant to speak.

"Well, the short answer is nothing. No records, remember? If you die you become part of the Valley. Eh, there are worse places."

\*\*\*

Pilot Bob had an intuitive sense of the land. He guided the plane with the same subconscious focus as I did traveling the almost straight highway between Mom's house and mine. Snow dotted the cockpit windshield as we neared our destination.

"You're takin' a risk bein' up here this early. Snow can fall any month of the year, but you don't really see the bad stuff in the summer when the tourists hit. If it feels dangerous, just move into the Valley and find shelter. Plenty of caves and overhangs," Pilot Bob said.

"What about bears?" Oscar asked, one hand on the spray hooked to his belt.

Pilot Bob laughed, "If you find one sleepin' leave 'im be, eh? Speaking of that, it's gonna be more dusky than dark at night this time of year. Some struggle with it. If you can't sleep at night try to nap during the day."

"Where are you gonna land?" Oscar asked.

Below us, the trees had thickened into a green sea, and it was just as endless. Small peaks erupted here and there like frozen waves.

"I know a spot," Pilot Bob said. "You're not close to anythin' you seen on the Internet. But that's what you're lookin' for, eh? To see something you never seen before? You'll find it. I promise."

As the plane descended, Pilot Bob guided it to the west. There was a strip of white fracturing the sea of trees. Too narrow, it seemed. My elbows touched my thighs as I braced for the inevitable crash. The landing felt like a series of them, the tundra tires springing the plane back into the air several feet. I kept the motion sickness at bay throughout the flight but felt the familiar spread of lukewarm petals at the base of my neck, the tightening of my belly as Pilot Bob wrestled the plane to a stop.

"We're here," he said, seeming almost surprised at that result.

We deplaned and offloaded the gear. The wind slapped my cheeks, numbing them with icy hands. Perhaps July would have been better. Oscar rejected the idea in the planning stage.

"I'm not goin' all that way to make friends," he had said.

I understood. I thought I did. It was like he was determined to make up for all the memories we did not create. To pack a life's worth of adventure into a single week.

"I'll be right here seven days from now, this time give or take a couple hours. Now, time can get…away from you in the Valley. Might seem odd, but you'd be doin' yourself a favor to write down the day each morning. Just make a note of it somewhere."

I nodded for the group as Oscar and Gillian were facing the Valley to the north and east. The landmarks Pilot Bob mentioned were broken hockey sticks painted orange, spaced about two hundred feet apart. Not that we needed them to find the Valley. There wasn't a physical demarcation establishing its limits, just the gradual slope of the terrain leading into canyons.

"Make noise. Worst thing you can do is sneak up on something hungry, eh? Next worst thing you can do is run. That's like throwing a bone to a dog. Stand your ground if you need to but be respectful. The Valley isn't your home. You're just passin' through. You're a guest in someone else's home. Treat it that way. Treat it with respect."

Pilot Bob extended a gloved hand to shake. I took it, attempted to squeeze but couldn't feel much through my own glove.

"Tomorrow is day two. Remember that. And if you only hear one thing I tell you, let it be this…the most dangerous animal in that place is you."

He stood beside the plane and just breathed. The flapping sound I heard was not a bird, as I thought, but a strip of duct tape coming loose from the wing. The realization hit me then. What if Pilot Bob died? Either in an accident or from a thousand other possibilities in consideration of his age and habits. The previous night's libations were not celebratory in nature, I gathered. He drank like that every day. Who would know to look for us? Did the folks in Fort Simpson know when we were supposed to return? Before I could ask him this or any other question, he was back inside his plane squinting at the instrument panel.

In an emergency, loss of life, limb or eyesight, we were to head east. He pointed vaguely. There was a ranger station that was likely unmanned. He said we would hear the roar of Virginia Falls long before we reached it, and that sound would guide us. There we would find provisions as well as a radio.

"If you use that radio and mention my name," he said, then dragged a thumb across his neck.

The plane eased away, the buzz of its engine throttling my eardrums. I gritted my teeth and turned. Oscar and Gillian abandoned the small mountain of gear to join me. The plane picked up speed, skipping over the earth until it caught wind and began to rise just before the makeshift, or possibly accidental, runway terminated.

"Well, guess we start walkin'," Oscar said, pointing to a broken hockey stick visible between evergreens.

Though not cold by north Canada standards, it was colder than I was accustomed to. My military career took me all over the world but rarely further north than Virginia. I tugged my beanie lower and followed my brother. The path was slick, a fresh inch of snow camouflaging a much thicker layer of ice just beginning to soften. We passed seven hockey sticks before the trees began to noticeably space out, small boulders interrupting the landscape, clusters of green emerging from the snow and ice.

"I think we're getting close," Oscar said, his breath just shy of labored.

And there it was. Had something in the sky caught his attention he would have tumbled into the canyon. Instead, he skidded to a halt, arms splayed for balance.

"Holy shit," he whispered.

I have replayed the moment many times. The moment before. One of the final moments of not knowing. I remember the breath dropping out of my lungs, my mind warring against the information relayed by my eyes. I didn't have the words for it then. I have never found them.

He perched a hand on his hip, draped an arm over my shoulder.

"I can't believe it," I said. "I can't believe it's real."

Oscar's previous recollection was accurate. I was a voracious reader but a rarely satisfied one. There wasn't enough for me. There wasn't enough information, enough wonder. Reading about the discoveries made only a few generations ago made me feel as if I was born outside of my rightful time. I had the diaries of dead men; they had a horizon without limits.

Gillian rested her cheek on my opposite shoulder. I did not shy away from the gesture because I did not sense desperation behind it. She was my oldest friend. There were others from school and the Air Force. Some I kept up with on social media. But none knew me like her.

"I'm glad I'm here with you," she said, like waking up from a dream.

I was glad, too. But I didn't say it.

I felt the wind of Oscar's abrupt departure, sharp as the crack of a whip. He stood above another precipice twenty feet away, body angled toward distant snowy peaks, elbow aimed at me like an oversized arrow.

\*\*\*

Pilot Bob advised we set up camp above the Valley.

*If somethin' gets in your camp and you gotta run, better to have the option of goin' down than bein' forced to climb. You're not built for it.*

We straddled the rim of the Valley and found an overhang with enough space for both tents and a campfire. Oscar wanted to set up camp after exploring but Gillian made a good point.

"You think we're gonna have the energy to set up tents after hiking for hours?"

Oscar scratched the back of his neck, "Yeah. You're right. I just hate dealing with tents. That was the worst part of being in the Army."

"Should've joined the Air Force. I've never been within a half mile of a tent," I said.

"Funny."

Working as a team, Oscar and I were still several minutes behind Gillian, who sat with her legs dangling above the Valley as we fought the tent poles.

"It doesn't look dangerous," she said.

I managed to work up a sweat despite the chilly temperature and wiped a gloved thumb across my brow.

"What's that?" I asked.

"The Valley. It doesn't look dangerous. It looks… magical."

After pounding in the final stake, I joined her at the edge of the overhang. The Valley lunged upward, a touch of vertigo forcing me to my knees. I placed a hand on her shoulder to steady myself.

"You okay, J?" she asked.

I was never great with heights. Once when we were kids, Oscar convinced me to climb on the roof of our house. It was summer, and Mom worked two jobs then. Meaning, she didn't get home until the evening. When she did, I was still on the roof, lips like shed snakeskin, nose as red as an overripe pepper. Oscar was hiding in the bathroom, rightfully afraid Mom would blame him.

"Yeah. Just had a moment. I'm good."

"You ready?" Oscar asked.

"I am," Gillian said, standing and dusting herself off.

"Lead the way, Bro," I said.

\*\*\*

The Valley of the Headless Men was not a single valley. It was a vast expanse of canyons and rivers, skyscraping granite towers shaped by the last ice age. I did not know if we were near the open-air tombs of the Valley's namesake beheaded men. My Internet research into the topic did not mention proximity among the discovered bodies. Were the deaths and beheadings localized or spread out? The answer to that question could suggest something about the nature of their deaths.

"I wonder if they saw who did it," I said.

Oscar was about fifteen feet ahead, left leg straight but skidding as we descended to the Valley floor. We grabbed saplings and exposed tree roots, the ground beneath our boots like shifting sand.

"They?" he grunted.

"The headless men. Whatever killed them...did it do it from behind or while they were asleep?"

"I think I'd rather die in my sleep. If I'm gonna lose my head, I mean. I'd rather my dreams just darken to nothing," Gillian said.

"Is that what you think happens? Nothing?" I asked.

I paused, boot braced against a tree root. The Valley floor was near. I thought I could make it if I pushed off and just started running.

"I don't know. I like that idea of reconciling your mistakes and trying again."

A small avalanche preceded the fluttering tattoo of Gillian's boots as she rocketed past me, arms like the wings of an airplane. She passed Oscar next, her momentum carrying her a further fifty feet over the Valley floor. Oscar looked up at me. His brow was shiny with sweat, rapid puffs of mist obscuring his features as he struggled to catch his breath.

"Aren't you military guys?" Gillian called. "This should be easy."

"I was!" Oscar yelled. "I got fat!"

He was stout, not fat, but neither of us were in our old fighting shape. I almost let go and ran, but the idea of a week at the top of the world with a broken tibia tempered my bravado. A decade ago, just past the halfway point of my military service, I injured my ankle on a ruck march. Bad enough I was sent home early from that deployment and nearly medically separated. Had Oscar been in my life then, I'm sure he would have delighted in his Air Force brother sustaining an almost career-ending injury on what was a typical Saturday afternoon for him.

Oscar reached the Valley floor with a hop and a skip. He sprawled but popped up like a prairie dog, backpack hanging off one shoulder. I skidded to the next sapling, kicked off a half-buried boulder and my momentum did the rest.

The world was at the mid-morning of its day. Meaning, it had cast off the shackles of winter, of long, quiet nights only interrupted by the sound of tired branches succumbing to the weight of snow. Wildflowers trembled moth-wing petals toward the sun. I did not know the names of the flowers, only that I had never seen them before. They were mostly pale, moon-shades, but striped with pinks and purples. The air thrummed with the buzzing of bees, thumb-sized and with furry, pollen-dusted coats.

Though the land was rousing there was a strange stillness, like a movie set after the crew has retired and only the scenery is left behind. It was too beautiful, too immense. I felt no bigger than the bees bobbing past my ankles. The sense of overwhelm bled the strength from my knees. My lungs ached from the cold, clean air. I never wanted to see another sky, to breathe other air than this. I understood why Pilot Bob stayed.

Had my father stood here or somewhere nearby? Did he make it this far, or was it only a passing interest?

The joy swelling in my chest found an anchor, dropping it into my stomach and chilling it to ice. He traveled, or wished he had, to the end of the world. He went that far for himself. He raised children that did not share his blood...

"It's a lot, isn't it?" Oscar said.

"Hm? Oh, yeah."

"Thinkin' about him?"

"Didn't mean to. How can you tell?"

"Got that same far-off stare. Just like when you were little."

Oscar's gloved hand stroked the stubble of his cheek, the middle finger lingering over the scar his father had given him. He didn't tell the truth about the injury for years. Instead, he went along with father's story, that he tripped and caught the edge of the coffee table. I was five then, too young to understand but not too young to notice. Oscar would go quiet as a weekend with his dad approached, staring at the front door from the living room for twenty, thirty straight minutes. I asked him about it later, after his dad stopped coming around. He said if he stared at the door long and hard enough, his mind would play tricks on him. The black line between the door and the frame would fade. The door would become a wall, one his dad could not pass through. It didn't work while we were little, but he kept trying.

"Do you hear the water?" Gillian asked.

"That's what it is! I don't trust my hearing anymore. Too many days on the range. But I knew there was somethin'," Oscar said.

"Care to lead?" I asked.

"I prefer it," she said with a wink.

\*\*\*

The further we got from the shadows of the canyon walls the less snow we encountered. The pillowed earth beneath our boots was spongy with new grass, the snow and ice surviving only in dwindling patches.

"It's so goddamn beautiful I feel like humming," Oscar said.

"How about a frolic?" Gillian teased.

"I don't have the knees for frolicking. If you wanna see a brown man snap in two I can make that happen."

The drone of rushing water took shape, little intricacies emerging from white noise like a pattern recognized in static. I walked forward but my attention was pulled to either side of me. The canyon wall to my left where we caught a fleeting glimpse of a Dall Sheep disappearing among trembling aspen. To my right, new species of wildflowers dotted the meadow like miniature fireworks. The sun burned the edges off the cold, our breaths no longer visible. After half an hour of walking in mostly silence, my jacket was unzipped and my gloves tucked in a pocket.

I did not know I needed this when I submitted to my brother's wishes. Half my life was behind me, and that story was already written. Ahead were blank pages mostly disconnected from those preceding. Gillian was there. So was Oscar. They were two carryovers from the first half of the story, and I was happy to have them.

A zebra-stripe pattern of shadows and white birch formed a wall along the water source we sought. Why follow the sound of rushing water? What else was there to do? We had no agenda beyond exploring, no limits beyond our physical and navigation capabilities.

The meadow led to a patch of tightly packed sand, darker where the river water had recently overflowed its banks. Pilot Bob warned the water would be fierce. Snow from higher elevations would melt well into summer. Streams joined rivers, eroding the banks by inches, enough to liberate the soil crowding roots of trees and send them toppling.

There was a log on the sand long enough to accommodate the three of us. Gillian led us there but was not ready to rest.

"I wanna take pictures," Gillian said, setting her backpack on the sand and squatting to rummage through it.

"Take some for all of us," Oscar said.

He dropped his backpack and groaned as he sat. I followed suit but turned my moan into a sigh. Gillian was already gone, her boot prints aiming toward the stream. I massaged my ankle without thinking about it but couldn't feel the pressure through the thickness of the boot.

"Is it like you thought it would be?" I asked. If he had posed the same question, I would have said *no*. I did not know this beauty existed in the world. Tales of headless men and secret caverns to the inner-Earth were insignificant compared to the real wonder surrounding me.

His head was tilted to the side. I could not see his eyes. After a few seconds passed I wondered if he had fallen asleep. Rather than answer, he unzipped his backpack and withdrew a sheathed knife. He stood, the knife at his side, his back to me. His shoulders were slumped, head downcast. My fingers tingled. I swallowed and checked my surroundings. Old training instincts coming back to me.

"Oscar?"

He had not mentioned the knife. It was logical to have one considering the environment, but it was strange to keep it secret.

"You okay, Bro?" I asked, my hands braced on the log. The word, bro, felt strange in my mouth.

He turned performatively, inches at a time. His eyes were on my boots, the knife an afterthought in his hand.

"Sorry. Just…got lost in my own mind. You know how it is."

He said the words carefully and quietly. Then, with the same slow deliberation, he snapped the sheath to his belt opposite the bear spray.

"I'm not following," I said.

Oscar sat beside me, the gap between us wider than it had been moments ago.

"This wasn't the last time he hit me," Oscar said, tapping the scar above his cheek. "I think it scared him. I had to get stitches, remember? Fuckin' two days before school picture day. I went along with his story, though. Mom suspected. She asked me about it like I might slip up and…well, I guess there wasn't much she could do."

I searched for Gillian among the trees.

"Scared him enough that he stopped with the obvious stuff. No more blood. No. He'd pinch the soft places you couldn't see, twist my ear until I could hear the cartilage squeak like Styrofoam. Even when we were in church. Any little abuse he could get away with. A poke or a pinch. He'd shove me around the apartment, but not near the furniture."

"Oscar…"

He looked at me and winked, "That's okay, though. He's dead now, and you had your own…stuff."

I swallowed, "Why are you telling me this?"

He shrugged, "That's why we're here, isn't it? To shit on our dads?"

There was a shift in his tone, a flatness to it. It didn't feel like shitting on his dad. He grinned when he said the word *stuff*. It wasn't a scar beneath my eye, a bruise on my elbow or an ear that hurt to sleep on at night. He stood, unsheathed the knife, and began to walk toward the trees. A curious thought bloomed. Oscar was going to kill Gillian. Why would I think that about my own brother? He was not a violent man. Not to my knowledge. Still, I found myself reaching for a fist-sized rock on the sand.

I called his name and he stopped, turned and smiled. It was a real smile, one that made his scar disappear. He plunged the knife into the earth, then showed me the wrapper that must have fallen out of Gillian's bag.

"Pilot Bob is halfway to Fort Simpson by now, and he's the closest person to us in the world," Oscar said.

\*\*\*

Gillian found a clear spot on the riverbank, the current having claimed trees too close to the water. All that remained was a sapling tempting the same fate. The chaos of fallen trees was smoothed by the river, the sand as hard as concrete. She squatted there, her camera aimed at the opposite bank. Beyond it, like a ghost, a granite tower loomed, its blunted peak wreathed in clouds.

As we approached, she held up a finger but did not lower her camera. Oscar stopped and I did as well, shielding my eyes and squinting across the water. The sunlight reflecting off the river was dazzling, a thousand sparks turning the world electric blue.

"Shit," Gillian whispered, standing up and stretching her legs.

"What?" Oscar said.

"There was a moose. I only saw the antlers. They were so small, and he was so still I thought it was a log or something."

"They're dangerous, aren't they? Didn't Bob say something about them killing more people than bears?" I said.

"Might be taking car crashes into account. And I think they are dangerous, yes, but more dangerous during the rut.

Right now, they're probably too focused on eating to notice us," Oscar said.

"Still don't wanna spook one," Gillian said.

"That's true. Although I'm guessing if this spray can stop a bear, it can probably stop a moose," Oscar said.

"If I get killed by a moose, I want you to tell everyone it was a bear. A big one," I said.

Gillian nodded, perhaps not sensing my attempt at humor.

"Did you get any pictures?" I asked.

Gillian checked the camera screen, the frown on her face not wavering, "Nothing that resembles a moose. Just some brown that could be anything."

"There any place to cross over?" Oscar asked.

Gillian shielded her eyes and pointed, "Might be. Further up if it narrows. There are fallen trees but haven't seen any that look stable enough to cross."

Gillian rejoined us and we took turns pivoting and pretending to know what to do next. There were trails to follow, but none in our area of the Valley. Oscar specifically wanted an uncorrupted experience. He could not tolerate the knowledge of other visitors, of walking a well-trodden path. We were left to create our own trails.

"Let's follow the river. See if it changes," I said.

"Into what?" Oscar asked.

"Maybe there's a waterfall. The water comes from somewhere, right? And if we stick to the river, we can find our way back."

Oscar nodded. He was all smiles again, "You're so smart, Bro. That's why you were in those gifted classes, huh?"

We kept the river on our right, sometimes migrating away as the land softened into boot-sucking marsh. The valley widened, the western canyon wall angling away from us. Back at Fort Simpson and about five drinks in, Pilot Bob told me I would notice it eventually.

"Notice what?" I asked.

"When the Valley notices *you*."

"How can it notice me?"

He stared so long I thought he might not answer. In retrospect, I think he was reflecting, recalling the same moment for himself.

"You've felt it before. Everyone has. When you feel it again, you'll know."

I noticed many things, but the Valley was oblivious to me. The sun seemed small and far away, not like Texas. Wildlife lingered in the periphery, revealed by a branch bobbing absent any wind, a cascade of rocks tumbling like thrown dice. Mostly, it was quiet, a waiting sort of quiet, unhurried.

We followed the river for half an hour and might have covered a mile in distance due to the changing conditions of the terrain. Oscar was in the lead but not leading, whistling but not a song I recognized. After a few minutes in which no words were exchanged, he stopped.

"Look at that," he said, more to himself.

Gillian and I made up the short distance and stood to either side of him.

The river, which might have met the technical definition of a stream, disappeared. Fog as thick as sheep's wool interrupted the landscape like a god's discarded blanket. I noticed it then, as Pilot Bob predicted. There were no new thoughts in my mind. It gathered in my stomach, a little storm cloud sprouting tendrils. One tapped my heart and demanded a faster beat. Others explored my extremities. The wall of fog felt like a barrier, the Valley's *do not pass* sign. Gillian stepped forward, and I grabbed her elbow reflexively.

There was a strange tension in being friends. Twenty years ago, I would have walked through fire to protect her and the life growing in her belly. I told myself that, anyway. She said, jokingly in front of friends but earnestly during the long, slow hours of the night, that both being Geminis we were two halves of the same soul. She would remind me of the many ways we complement each other, our strengths and shortcomings evenly matched.

"Do you think it's possible?" she would whisper, fingers walking over my chest. "We were one soul that made a different choice?"

"I wish I could believe that stuff. Life would be so much more interesting," I would whisper back, taking her hand into mine.

My instincts warmed my blood and the world felt hyper-clear. More *real* than it had been seconds ago. What right did I have to stop her? She was my friend. Only my friend. She lifted her elbow until my fingers slid free.

"You don't feel that?" I said, gesturing at nothing behind me.

*Feel what? s*he might have asked. I could not define it other than to explain the effect it had on my body, like suddenly realizing the gates to every enclosure in the zoo were open.

Instead, she responded with her own question, "You don't *hear* that?"

She cupped a hand around her ear and leaned forward then began to walk. I did not reach for her but followed behind, my boots only slightly overflowing the prints she left.

"I don't hear anything. Just the birds and the water. It's...quieter where the fog is. Maybe it's over a lake or something."

She shook her head and held up a finger, squinting as if to minimize the inputs of her other senses. Oscar unsheathed his knife. His forehead was dotted with sweat, red bandana forgotten in his hand, and he looked everywhere but at me.

"No. I hear something. You don't? You don't hear that?" Gillian said.

"I don't. What is it? What do you hear?"

Her boots squelched in muck growing soggier with each step. The world was as still as a painting. No bees. The bird songs distant and there was no indication of their source.

My job in the Air Force was not combat-oriented. Most aren't. But that did not mean combat could not find me.

During my final deployment I was in a convoy traveling to FOBs, Forward Operating Bases, small outposts with little infrastructure, to check the status of medical equipment. At the third FOB, the convoy left without us. Some escort mission I wasn't tracking. We were told they had just left. If we hurried, we could catch them.

Four hours later, the truck's gas gauge was showing empty, and we were lost in Afghanistan. No comms. Not even a map. That's what it felt like approaching the wall of fog. We shouldn't be there. This space was not for us.

"Looks like you could just...scoop it up with your hands," Gillian said.

"Looks like the shit you see in horror movies," Oscar added.

It was gray like an oyster and almost still. Oscar probed it with his knife, and the fog coiled around the tip like a boa constrictor before dissipating. Gillian tilted her body away from my brother. She scanned my face before mouthing the words *do you hear it?*

I shook my head again. There were many sounds at the time, all of them subtle and none seemingly from within the fog. She nodded, coming to terms with a decision she did not articulate, then entered the fog.

"Gillian!" I shouted, the name reflecting back at me as if the fog was a mountain.

"I'm okay," she said, her voice muddier and fainter than it should have been. "Just give me a second. It's really close."

"What is?"

Beside me, Oscar held his knife out as if he expected a brown bear to emerge in Gillian's place. His sweat was a torrent, ears red not from cold but overheating.

"Oscar," I said, and he glanced at me without turning his head. "You look sick, man. Are you okay?"

He didn't answer. His focus was on the fog and whatever it might be hiding.

Ten seconds passed. Thirty.

"Gillian!"

No answer.

"Give me the knife!" I hissed. His eyes narrowed as he rocked back and forth like a boxer before the bell rings. "Oscar! Give me the fu-"

The fog parted and Gillian appeared. I opened my mouth to speak but the words got clogged in my throat as I followed her gaze to the object in her hand.

It couldn't be.

It couldn't be.

It couldn't...

"Gillian..."

She extended her arms like an offering. The baby monitor was the same model gifted to us by her parents two decades ago. It never transmitted his voice, only static as she triggered it at night, thinking I had fallen asleep.

"Did you..." I began, unwilling to commit myself to the thought.

She withdrew the offering, tucking it against her body. For a moment, her eyes were full of wonder, basking in the glow of a miracle. No more.

"I didn't bring it, Joseph," she said through clenched teeth. "Why would you..."

"I didn't. I...it just doesn't make sense. H- how is that thing here?"

Behind her, the wall of fog roiled. I looked to my brother for support.

"Oscar. Tell her it doesn't make sense."

He blinked a few times, glancing from the baby monitor to me. The knife was held out in front of him like a rotten banana destined for the trash can. His cheeks burned, dozens of droplets threatening to fall at the slightest movement.

"Oscar?"

The knife slipped from his fingers, the blade sinking in muck to the hilt.

"I don't feel-"

I lurched forward as he crumpled, cradling his head and we fell together.

***

Gillian was no longer with us. Not mentally. She followed behind like a child only halfway paying attention. What led her to the baby monitor was a voice, she said, but we heard only static.

Static. How did we even hear that? It was impossible. The wall of fog was impossible. The baby monitor was impossible.

"I think I'm good to walk on my own, Bro."

Oscar claimed he was dehydrated, that he had not replenished properly after vomiting twice the evening before. It was logical, but also not the whole story. There was something else happening, revealed in tiny agitations. My ankle was grateful to be relieved of the burden of his weight, though.

"You sure?"

"Yeah, just need to get some electrolytes in me. I brought that powdered stuff. It's back at the camp."

"You want this back?" I asked, patting my backpack. The knife was secured next to my water bottle.

"Uh, you can hang onto it."

The static was fainter. Behind, Gillian had wandered off-course. I called her name and she adjusted but did not look up from the baby monitor. She held the trigger down and spoke, not loud enough for me to hear, then pressed the speaker to her ear.

*Whatever you think is happening, Gillian. It isn't.*

What brought me here was not something I believed in. There were no giants, no hidden herd of mammoths thriving in the park while leaving no trace. The deaths of long-ago trappers and treasure hunters might have been real. They might also have been a clever way to limit competition. Though fascinated by the legends I was agnostic to them, and more focused, in the near-term, on the states of mind of my companions. When Nahanni began to show itself, the veil thinning enough to see unnatural silhouettes, I burrowed into that agnosticism. This was day one. Day one at the edge of the world with nothing to stop us if we fell.

***

By my watch it was nearly 9 PM. I would have guessed we were in the Valley for three or four hours, but it had been eight since Pilot Bob dropped us off. Regret settled in. Behind me, Oscar was chewing his fingernails and sweating like we were in a sauna. His bandana, wet and useless, hung from his pocket. Behind him, Gillian was whispering to a baby monitor.

The terrain looked familiar. We were near the area Gillian spotted the elusive moose. In half an hour we would reach our camp. Maybe things would begin to feel normal there, above the Valley. I was out of water and my feet screamed as if there were wasps in my boots.

"Is that...smoke?" Gillian said, the baby monitor at her side rather than her ear for the first time since she found it.

I followed the direction of her gaze. Yes, there was smoke, a thin, steady stream of it in the general direction we headed.

"Is our...camp on fire?" Oscar mumbled.

"I don't think so. No way that could have happened. I mean...no way that makes sense," I said. "Can't be a brush fire, though. It's too narrow and steady."

"Okay," Gillian said, then returned her attention to the baby monitor.

The smoke was a steady feature on our horizon, never changing in thickness or color. We lumbered at a zombie's pace, saying little. Half an hour passed, the sky not darkening but changing colors. My hamstrings twitched, threatening to seize. We'd probably covered ten miles by then, not a staggering number except the ground underfoot wasn't solid. More like walking on marshmallows.

"There's a person. It's a campfire, the smoke. Look, there's a person on that outcrop," I said as we neared it.

"No," Oscar grunted. "Can't be. There's not supposed to be anyone here. It's just supposed to be us."

# CHAPTER FIVE

Nautical twilight is when the sun dips below the horizon, its light streaked there like electric paint, before rising again a few hours later. It was never truly dark in Nahanni, not on the rim of it, but sleep still claimed me like a rising tide. The water proved to be shallow, however, as my consciousness was just beneath the surface. Bursts of static invaded my dreams, the lilting singsong of Gillian in the other tent.

I woke every half hour or so to the same sight of the back of Oscar's head. He said little upon returning to camp, grumbling about the presence of another person in the park, and fell asleep with his boots on while Gillian and I were debating getting a fire started. We abandoned the effort, ate food without warming it up, and stumble-crawled into our tents like bears with swollen bellies and dreams of winter.

It was only six AM but bright as midday. I blinked at Oscar's sleeping bag, convinced my eyes were playing tricks as it appeared to be black. I pressed my hand down on it and found it was not black. It was saturated with sweat. I had seen him like this before. Remembered his sheets so yellowed they looked like coffee stains. Before I could consider the implications, I heard a conversation outside of the tent. Two men.

"Oscar?" I said, wriggling out of my sleeping bag. Where was the knife?

I unzipped the tent flap and was confronted by blinding daylight filtered through the twitching needles of evergreens. Between me and Oscar was a man, the color washed out of his clothes due to the sunlight flaring across my vision. He turned at the sound of my voice, and for a moment, for the space between heartbeats, I thought it was my father.

*Dad?* I almost spoke the word, but he took a step forward and blocked the sunlight. I last saw my father in person when he was in his mid-thirties, a picture maybe five years after that. His new family stood behind him, two girls and a boy whose handwriting he did not haunt. This man was not him. Even that moment of uncertainty was embarrassing in retrospect. The man was my age, or perhaps a few years younger. The hair dusting his shoulders was either auburn or pecan brown depending on the intensity of the sun. Dad's hair was coal black and within military regulations even after retirement.

"Good morning!" the man said, bending over with a hand extended.

His smile was so wide and genuine I took the offered hand without question. It was not the smile of a first meeting but of a reunion with a close friend, a brother. Our hands united, he pulled me up to a standing position with surprising strength considering his frame.

"Good morning..." I trailed off.

"Sam. Nice to meet you, Joseph. Been chatting with your brother for a few minutes. He told me about how you came to this place. Quite a journey!"

"Yeah...it's been...an experience. How did you get here? I thought the-"

*Kzzzttt*

Gillian emerged from her tent, the baby monitor pressed to her chest. Angry capillaries burst from her pupils like little crackles of red lightning. Plum-dark half-moons pulsed beneath her eyes.

"And good morning to you!" Sam said, offering his hand again. "It's so wonderful to make new friends."

Gillian turned her body away as if hiding the baby monitor from the stranger.

"It's okay. He's a veteran. A *Nahanni* veteran I mean. He's been here...how many times was it?" Oscar said.

"Oh, I don't know the true number. It feels like my second home if that helps to paint the picture," Sam replied.

It still didn't make sense to me. Neither did Oscar's suddenly cheerful disposition. When we spotted the man the evening prior Oscar was annoyed if not furious.

"Sam knows about the Valley. He knows where to take us," Oscar said, the emphasis placed on certain words implying the knowledge was not common. Not something we could have found online or in a book.

"Oh yeah?" I said, appraising the newcomer again.

He was about my height and dressed like a scarecrow. A plaid shirt open to the middle of his torso, sleeves rolled up. His jeans flared at the bottom over mud-caked sneakers. No hiking boots? After slip-sliding down the canyon leading into the Valley there was little actual hiking, more of a nature walk. Still, the descent was treacherous, and *nature* included mud that stuck to our boots like peanut butter.

"You wanted an experience? She'll give it to you. We're not far from the cabin if that's something that interests you."

What interested me was how this man made it to Nahanni. Bob said we would be alone, likely in the entire park and certainly in that part of it. Perhaps there was another rogue pilot flying out of Yellowknife. The questions piled up in my mind, but I held onto them. I did want an experience. My mind crafted explanations for the wall of fog, the somehow functioning baby monitor. There were hot springs in the park, the air around them mild enough to support ferns that would not look out of place in the Everglades. Hot springs meeting chilly air was the perfect environment for fog. The baby monitor functioned like a walkie-talkie. Maybe it was used for that purpose.

"The cabin?" Gillian said. "What's that?"

Sam shook his head, beaming like a jack o' lantern, "Won't make sense to explain it to you. It *is* a cabin. That part makes sense. But it's not *just* a cabin. Not always."

"Not always? What does that mean?" I asked.

Sam winked, "You should go first. Tell us what it means."

*Lead the way*, I almost said. But Oscar spoke first as he patted his belly.

"After breakfast. Ol' Oscar almost ran out of gas yesterday."

\*\*\*

Sam led us down a different path into the Valley, almost like natural switchbacks. Maybe that's why he wore sneakers instead of hiking boots. It did make the descent easier and added credibility to the claims Sam made or were made on his behalf by a smitten Oscar.

The air was colder than the day before, our exhalations perpetually swirling around our faces like ectoplasm. It ached in my lungs, a dull knife attempting to rupture my chest from the inside. By the time we reached the Valley floor, the sun was hidden behind a shapeless canopy of clouds.

"Think it'll snow?" Oscar asked as we waited for Gillian to meet us on the grass.

Sam glanced skyward for a moment, hands on his hips as if considering the question in earnest, "Weather here is hard to predict. Been surprised by a blizzard before I had time to throw a jacket on. That's the way it usually goes, huh? You never get surprised by it turnin' warm all of a sudden. It's always cold."

Gillian approached, ear pressed to the baby monitor's speaker. Since discovering it she might have spoken a few dozen words.

"You're not from here, are you? From Canada."

"Well, I never stayed in one place long enough to grow roots. I'm more of a lost kite, you know? Goin' where the wind blows me," Sam said, then beckoned. "I haven't been to the cabin since the last time I was in Nahanni. We'll try the direct path first but might get turned around if the water's too high."

He did not linger for further questioning but established a rapid pace, weaving around foliage like a fox. Oscar was on his heels, peppering him with questions I only caught fragments of. My brother was recharged, focused. That was good, but it didn't feel that way. Sam wore no backpack. He had no gear beyond the belt fighting to keep his jeans from sliding past his hips. If the weather was as unpredictable as he suggested, he was prepared only for the current conditions. Rain or snow would have posed a serious problem.

Oscar's words lost clarity as I slowed to grow the distance between us. It wasn't Sam's attire, the apparent lack of preparation. It was knowing he should not be there, that we should not be following him. Beyond the color of his shirt and jeans there was nothing about him I could prove to be true.

The terrain rolled in small hills just steep enough to set fire to my quads. Where the ground leveled pockets of forest thrived, mostly trees so skinny I could encircle them with two hands. There were bushes of bright red berries that would have looked at home within the frosting mortar of a witch's gingerbread house. A silly idea, and maybe a message from my subconscious. How many fairy tales involved the sudden appearance of a smiling stranger?

"What do you think?" I asked Gillian.

She jolted, surprised at my presence as her focus had been on the baby monitor.

"About?"

I pointed.

"I don't know, Joe. He seems friendly enough, just..." she said, then gestured at the environment surrounding us. I understood the implication. We were supposed to be alone. If we misunderstood that fact, then meeting Sam was a happy accident. We had a guide tailor-made for the experiences we sought. If we did not, if the yellow fear twisting in my belly was a premonition...

Her eyes drifted to the baby monitor. She evaded my questions about it, not that she could have answered them.

"What does it mean? If it means anything. If it isn't some random junk left by a camper."

Gillian turned the knob and the static increased in volume. After a few seconds she turned it down.

"I don't know yet. I- I swore it wasn't static I heard. I probably wouldn't have noticed static among all the other noise. Water rushing, you know? It was a voice. Not words. But a voice."

"Did you recognize it?"

Her lips rolled inward, and her nostrils flared. She averted her eyes as if fearing I would judge her tears.

"I think so, Joe. I think so."

"Yeah?"

"I'll tell you once I'm sure."

I thought of the cold, silent room. The sound of a baby testing its lungs nearby as our son lay still as a stone in the crook of her arm. A nurse walked in, her eyes scrutinizing the tiles under her squeaky shoes. Without uttering a single word of condolence, she wheeled away the equipment that monitored his heart in utero. The world was moving on. Our son died without a name, and the world could not forget him quick enough.

*You never heard his voice, Gillian. Maybe in a dream, but never in life. And he was too young...*

Maybe it was another voice, but I didn't think so. Gillian arched her eyebrows and nodded in lieu of pointing. Oscar and Sam had disappeared beyond a rise in the terrain. She jogged to catch up and I fell in line behind.

\*\*\*

We crossed what Sam told us was a tributary of the river we encountered the day before. There was a boulder in its center, close enough to the shore we could reach it in a leap. Its surface was flat and dry. Sam bounded across with the grace of a mountain goat, seeming to hover over the stone rather than step off it. After a few false starts that almost sent him tumbling into the water, Oscar managed to leap onto the boulder, collect himself, and land safely on the other side. Gillian placed the baby monitor in her backpack, the first time I'd seen it out of her hand since its discovery. Not holding it motivated her to move quickly, as she was across and unzipping her backpack in the space of a single breath.

Sam led Oscar away, the pair now walking side-by-side.

"It's easier than it looks," Gillian said with a wink.

I was glad to see her smile return, the monitor forgotten for the moment at her hip.

"Not worried about easy. Just don't wanna be the only one to take a spill. It'd be a long, cold walk back to camp."

I had forgotten the pain in my ankle until that moment. I didn't trust myself to plant on my dominant foot, and also did not trust my left leg to be coordinated enough. The jump was ugly. I could feel that in the air, but I didn't fall. Gillian and I followed the trail of flattened grass and wildflowers, Oscar and Sam flashing into view every half minute or so.

"Is it like you thought it would be?" I asked.

"Nahanni?"

"Yes. Technically, you invited yourself. I had my guesses as to why, but we didn't really talk about it."

"Mmmmhmm, and what were your guesses?"

"To get away. To see something new," I lied.

*To be alone with me.*

The way Gillian looked at me I thought I'd spoken the words out loud. My heart felt like a butterfly in a spider's web.

"To let go."

Her tone was too flat for me to guess her meaning.

"Let go of what?"

With her free hand, she explored the left pocket of her jeans.

"Joseph!" Oscar called. "It's here!"

I stopped and she did, too. Her hand emerged from the pocket, and it was empty. I thought, feared it might have been a picture of us or some other memento of our relationship. Not that I had ambitions of a future with her, but it was still an open door unless she closed it.

"You don't have to tell me," I said.

"I know I don't, Joe. It's just that, when you struggle with something for so long...progress might feel like a reset. Like starting over even if it's not."

"I'm not sure I follow."

"Come on!" Oscar yelled.

Gillian hooked her arm inside mine and pulled me forward, "Let's go before your brother bursts a blood vessel."

The vague response gnawed at me.

"Oscar can survive another minute. What do you mean by progress and a reset?"

She leaned her body into me, "You came here because of your dad. Partially, at least. I know you don't expect to find him or any evidence of him. Knowing your dad, he probably never followed through. That's what he was best at, right?"

"Yeah."

"You've been carrying your dad on your back for the past twenty years. I know you have, because if that letter had been from anyone but him you wouldn't have come. Is this progress in your journey or a setback?"

This trip was about Oscar, wasn't it? A new beginning for us as brothers?

"I guess I don't know the answer to that."

"Hmm. Is it Cheryl?"

"Cheryl?" I barked, almost coughing the word.

"What was she like, other than not liking me?"

What was Cheryl like? I had words in my back pocket, descriptors that didn't mean anything. Kind, yes but not always. Not toward the end. Loving, yes, selectively. She was not a pile of words, and why did Gillian need even those? To compare herself?

"I'm not sure how to answer that either."

"It's not a trick question, Joe. I'm not trying to steal you from her. And *steal* doesn't really apply anymore. I'm just curious. We never made it past a certain point. But you did with her."

*Why does it matter now?*

The trees thinned and we emerged into a clearing. The cabin was a hovel, constructed not with boards but with raw wood. It was maybe six feet long and a foot shy of that in width. The door was a flap of hide, gray in color like the wood. Though it was interesting to find any evidence of humanity, the structure was not impressive, likely offering protection only from the snow and a bit of wind.

"It's like the stories!" Oscar yelled. "That...Norwegian guy!"

Gillian turned up the volume of the monitor, maybe fearing she'd missed a transmission during our conversation. After listening for a second, she lowered the volume and winked at me, then relinquished my arm and studied the hovel.

"But didn't his cabin burn down?" she said.

In the muted shadows of nearby trees, the colors of Sam's flannel shirt and jeans were washed out, blending into the background. He stepped forward.

"There's a lot about the Valley you don't understand until you're here. We're not even in the thick of it. Just on the outskirts. It was a gamble to take you. If the cabin wasn't here, I'd have lost all credibility, huh?"

"What do you mean *if it wasn't here*?" I said.

He smiled again. I was beginning to hate it.

"Sometimes it isn't."

"Sometimes it isn't here?" Gillian said.

"Sometimes it isn't. But when it's here, it looks just like this," Sam said, patting the hide door flap. "Joseph, I think you're up first, right?"

Sam tugged the flap free of the twine fastening it to a knot in the wood of the doorframe.

"It's not much. I mean, I can see the whole inside from here." I said.

"It'll look different inside. Trust me."

Oscar reappeared on my right after a quick circuit around the cabin. He shrugged and gestured, "You first little bro."

Gillian separated herself from the group and squatted with her back turned. The baby monitor's blunted antenna peeked over her shoulder. There was no static, meaning she was speaking into it but too low for me to hear.

"Come on. It's what you're here for, right?" Sam said. His teeth were orange, blood leaking from the gums and mixing with his saliva. As if he saw himself through my eyes, he closed his mouth but continued smiling.

"You said the cabin isn't here sometimes. It disappears? What happens if it disappears when I'm inside?"

I did not believe the cabin disappeared. It was more likely Sam confused another area of the park with that one. The cabin was there whether or not Sam managed to navigate to it.

"Still don't believe, do you?"

"Believe what?"

His smile shrank and it changed the topography of his face. The dimples of his cheeks collapsed to hollows. He had no water, no food. He had only his clothes and his story. Who was this man?

"Just go inside, Joseph. Everything is what you make it. Believe or don't, but I really can't say more. I don't want to change it for you."

Sam inserted himself between me and Oscar. If Nahanni had its eye on me, I did not notice it then. I shrugged out of my backpack and propped it against the wall to the side of the door flap. It hung from its top left corner, twine looped through a hole in the hide and tied to another knot in the wood. I ducked, as the entrance required it, and saw nothing remarkable within. Nothing leftover.

"I don't see anything inside."

A hand on my shoulder.

"You're not *inside*," Sam said.

He shoved and I stumbled forward, grasping the hide as I fell. It slipped from my fingers, and I crashed to the dirt floor thick with brittle pine needles. Two steps would have been enough to reach the opposite side, but instead I was probing blindly. I whipped my head around expecting to see Sam grinning, expecting to see anything. The cabin was not constructed but pieced together. There was no mortar in the gaps, not even dried mud. It could not have been dark there, truly dark.

Instead of Sam there was black, as if he'd slammed a mausoleum door behind me. I yelled his name. My confusion tipped toward dread as my voice spread out around me like an empty gymnasium. There was too much space. I should have at least grazed the rough ceiling when I stood, but I didn't, and there was space above me. Too much space. The hovel, the cabin was smaller than the tent I shared with Oscar. I took a step forward, what I thought was forward. It could have been the opposite, moving away from the door and the people on the other side of it.

"Oscar?"

My voice took flight as I zombie walked, and my hands thrummed like struck piano strings. Five steps. Ten. Unless I was inadvertently walking in a tight circle, I should have touched a wall many times over. It was not darkness but blindness. Stretched out to infinity. I squeezed my hands into fists because I could do nothing else.

*What the fuck is happening?*

The wall of fog, the baby monitor, and now this. Did Sam know it would happen? Had he experienced it himself? He insisted I be the first to enter the cabin, shoving me to expedite the process.

The air was stuffy and coffin-hot. Sweat pasted my shirt to my torso.

"Os-scar w-where..." I said, my voice trapped below a whisper.

*skrik-skrik-skrik-skrik*

A gust snapped my shirt sleeves like a flag in a hurricane. I gasped, forearms crisscrossing in front of my face. I felt the movement of another body, the diminishing tremors of passing footsteps. I was not alone.

*A weapon. A weapon. I need a weapon.*

I patted my jeans, clawed at my spine searching for the backpack I knew was not there. I had only my hands and feet.

"What is this?"

My voice had the weight of a moth's wing.

*skrik-skrik-skrik-skrik*

Behind me now, my hair lifting in its wake. I did not know the appropriate word to assign it. A person? An animal? To my untrained ear, the footfalls were bipedal. That it came so near without touching me suggested it knew where I was. Maybe it adapted to this darkness. Maybe this was home.

I spun, grating the pine needles to sand beneath my boots. My face was oily with sweat. It coursed to my fingertips. Every breath felt like I had sucked it out of another man's lungs.

Lights, a pattern of lights in the distance. I disregarded the impossibility of that distance and walked toward it, compressing my body into the smallest shape possible. It was a tunnel, had to be. Sam had pushed me, and I descended without realizing it, somewhere beneath the cabin. That explained the darkness. The light I saw was the gaps between the wood, a beacon to the outside.

An old memory revived itself without thought, without formal acknowledgement or understanding. I felt it in my gut, a brief sense of weightlessness there. Acid singed my throat, but the memory burrowed deeper. I did not need words or pictures. My body remembered.

This was familiar, this ritual. I approached the light, the slats I knew were too even to be the shoddy wooden wall of the cabin. My innards shriveled as if repelled by the light, as if pulling me away from it.

It was a set of blinds. I knew exactly how the metal would feel beneath my fingertips. I knew the smell of dust, the musk of the curtains to either side of the window that hadn't been washed in a while. Mom picked up extra shifts when she could, and clean curtains weren't high on her priority list. There was a little white stool, two steps, beneath the window. I was too short to see through the blinds without it. Mom hid it from me once, put it under the sink in her bathroom, but I found it.

I knew what I would see. Before I parted the blinds, I knew what was outside the window. I could have drawn it from memory, though it was an image I tried to forget. It was a driveway, wide because the house was a duplex and we shared it with our neighbor. They were a young married couple, no kids, and they owned a maroon sedan. A Ford, but I never learned the model. Our half of the driveway was often unoccupied until the late evening. Judging by the brightness of the light it was earlier in the day. To the right there would be decorative bushes surrounded by wood chips that had to be refreshed every year because the sun bleached the color out of them. On the porch were white wicker chairs that screamed in a thousand voices when I sat on them.

I scaled the two steps and rested my chin where I had so many times before. I smelled the dust, the unwashed curtains. I felt the metal of the blinds between my fingers and parted them.

This was where I waited for my father.

Friday, sweating from my bus stop sprint, I would stand there with a backpack beside me stuffed with clothes and toys, R.L. Stines fresh from the school book fair. I saved them because Dad let me stay up late to read. He let me do things Mom didn't. I would rest my chin on the windowsill and stare through the parted blinds. Cartoons blare in the living room, interrupted by the occasional rattle of silverware as Oscar made sandwiches, two for him and one for me. He would knock before he entered and wait a moment in case I was crying.

"Can you watch?" I would say, descending the steps to eat the sandwich. Oscar would take my place, no stool needed. "I don't want to miss him if he comes."

It was kid logic. My father did not require I wait at the window for him, but I convinced myself it was necessary. Sometimes he did come, but the space between visits stretched in concert with the distance from the divorce. After a few months every other week became every third or fourth. If he didn't show up by six o'clock, he wasn't going to. But I manned my post because...

Because...

I parted the blinds knowing I would see the vacant half of our driveway, possibly a maroon sedan casting a shadow onto it. Instead, there was a station wagon, one I did not recognize. The sun blasted the windshield, hiding the driver behind a blinding reflection. There were figures in the backseat, three across, one in a booster. The car began to reverse. I saw the driver's hand grasp the headrest of the front passenger seat. Then I met eyes with a boy I did not know. At that distance I could not discern a color, but by his complexion I guessed they were lighter than mine. His hair was brown, not black, and it flopped over his forehead nearly touching his eyebrows.

We could have been the same age. The girl beside him sat a head shorter, only wisps of her hair visible. The toddler was a flurry of legs and arms.

The station wagon turned as it reversed, angling the windshield out of the sunlight. I saw him for just a moment, shadows underscoring the features I had not inherited. A dimple on his chin and a prominent brow. The woman to his right glanced out her window. Her face was plain, unremarkable, the same flat brown hair as the boy in the backseat.

This had never happened in life. The timing of it was wrong. When my father assumed that role in another family we were not living in the duplex. I was not small enough to require a stool.

The station wagon's brake lights flashed, and then Dad was gone.

What was it about them?

I swallowed and the blinds snapped closed.

What was it about me?

"It could be worse, Bro," Oscar said.

He smiled at me from the doorway of the playroom. Blood streaked the side of his face like war paint. It pulsed from a slit beneath his eye. He wore a Simpsons shirt that used to be his favorite. I found it months after the *accident*, balled up and hidden beneath his mattress. He told me it was spaghetti sauce.

"Oscar?"

He closed the door, and the light went with him.

There was no windowsill, no stool or blinds. I was alone again.

"Oscar!" I yelled. He could not be far away, in either reality I recently occupied.

*skrik...skrik...skrik*

Breath on my face. Coffee. His breath always smelled like coffee. I reached a hand out but pulled it back.

"Dad?" I whispered.

Another breath.

"If that's you, why are you doing this?"

Another breath.

I lifted my hand again. I tried to imagine what he would look like now. How would that feel beneath my fingertips? The dimple on his chin would be a good landmark. Everything else would have been warped by time.

I bridged what I thought was the distance between us, took one step and then another.

He wasn't there.

He never was.

\*\*\*

I processed time by the rumbling in my belly. The spike of adrenaline with no corresponding exertion alerted my body to the hunger I ignored upon waking. My tongue tasted like dirty keys. I walked through darkness not knowing if each step brought me closer to or further from my goal. The surface was flat, hard, compact dirt beneath a layer of pine needles.

Was it a vision or a dream? Had I accessed some event in the past, combining a moment I had not witnessed with the setting of the duplex? Or was it completely conjured?

The Valley's eyes were on me, like the tip of a knife tickling the hair of my neck. I walked faster, sweat like a second skin shifting over my form. My tongue sealed to the roof of my mouth. I could die there, wherever *there* was. I had no water and there were no sources of it.

I walked for what felt like hours, legs burning, the dirt becoming as unstable as sand beneath my boots. I pictured holes in my lungs, unable to hold the air I delivered to them. I had no plan and no presence of mind to form one. I could only walk and hope there was ground beneath my boots.

My feet tangled and I crashed to my knees. It felt better than walking. Maybe I would nap, just for a little while.

*tick-tick-tick*

Sweat dripped from the tip of my nose. Beneath me were tiny craters I could not see. Perhaps they would stay there, undisturbed by the weather, as my body eroded into elements, becoming nourishment for soil that would never harbor life. I would die thinking of my father, wondering about the choices he made and if my heart was a consideration within them.

\*\*\*

"Joe? What are you doing? Jesus how can you be so sweaty?"

Gillian stood in the doorway, face framed by a halo of light. The air was cold, and my sweat felt like ice melt.

"Gillian?"

Hours had passed since I considered the topography of the ground, how my death would not disturb the little craters.

"Yeah, Joe, what are you doing?"

I shielded my eyes, tried to stand but my legs were stones.

"How long has...how long have I been here?"

I could hear the smile in her voice but could not see her clearly.

"Are you joking? Like, ten seconds?"

"What?"

She retreated a step and the flap opened fully, more light spilling into the room. Gillian ducked her head to enter.

"Jesus, Joe, are you sick? She kneeled beside me and pressed the back of her hand to my forehead.

"Water?"

"Yeah, just a sec."

She unclipped her water bottle and passed it to me. I drank until my stomach ached, wiped my mouth and handed it back to her.

"Uh, yours is right outside if you need more. What happened?"

A shadow stretched across the room. Sam leaned inside and looked around as if seeing it for the first time.

"How was it, friend?"

There was blood on his teeth.

\*\*\*

The crackle of the campfire joined the static of Gillian's baby monitor. I heard them in stereo, as Gillian had retreated to her tent. Sam was gone as well, though I saw no smoke from his site. Oscar sat across from me, the flames sometimes climbing high enough to obscure his face.

"Do you remember making sandwiches for me?" I asked.

"What? Sandwiches?" he said, voice flattened by annoyance.

"When I would wait for my dad. Back when Mom had two jobs. Do you remember making sandwiches?"

Oscar scratched the inside of his elbow. His gaze was so placid I thought he might not respond.

He cleared his throat, "Why did it happen for you?"

I wasn't sure if we had moved on from sandwiches.

Oscar began to unbutton his shirt.

"I believe you. I believe it happened like you said. Why did it happen for you?"

"What do you mean, Oscar?"

He folded his shirt and placed it in his lap. His scratches were deep and slow.

"Your dad wasn't there for you. So what? Who fuckin' cares? Lots of deadbeats out there."

"It wasn't a *good* experience. We didn't have some...cosmic embrace across time. I saw the family he chose over me. I don't know if it was real or something I just made up, but it didn't feel good. The only good part was..."

Oscar stopped scratching his arm. In the low light and through flames I could see the angry red of his flesh.

"The only good part was what?"

"Was you. You bringing me a sandwich."

Oscar nodded. The static from Gillian's tent was replaced by her softly excited voice. I recognized the rhythm of her speech. She only got to practice it for a few months.

"Well, that's good I guess. Good for you."

\*\*\*

I don't know if I slept or just closed my eyes and dreamed. Time was irrelevant. I experienced a day's worth of time in the cabin, or wherever the cabin took me, and only seconds passed in reality. Beyond the tent it was perpetual twilight. Not day or night but on the precipice of either.

Oscar lay beside me, also not sleeping. I knew it because of his breaths. When you share a bed with someone for years, as we had as kids, those patterns become as familiar as the scent of your pillowcase. I sensed the strain in the air passing through his nostrils, felt the tension in his throat. While dreaming on the edge of sleep, I became aware of the sound of shifting fabric. Oscar was quietly, carefully snaking out of his sleeping bag. I watched with one half-lidded eye as he crouched by the tent's entrance, gripped the zipper, and tugged. Where was his knife?

Why would I think that?

He watched me, eyes lost in shadow. I breathed as if I was asleep. That knowledge, the normal cadence of a person's breath, was not mine alone. Three breaths passed before he was satisfied. He crawled outside, zipping the tent but not fully closed. There was a gap the size of my thumb.

I tracked his movements by sound. He waddled around the cold charcoal of the extinguished campfire and sighed as he sat. Oscar took care not to wake me, though I did not understand his motivation, if the courtesy was for me or him. Maybe while he lay beside me not sleeping, he reconsidered his attitude toward me.

In the cabin, Gillian helped me to my feet and through the doorway. I downed all the water in my bottle before telling my story. The room went black and then expanded. I did not understand the mechanism of it and could only explain the experience of wandering in darkness, sensing the presence of a hidden other, recognizing the blinds from my childhood. The stool, my dad and his new family. Oscar, bleeding from the eye. I didn't talk about that part.

My sweat was evidence of the hours I walked in darkness, calling for my brother, eventually giving up. I was glad to see him, but he side-stepped my embrace. Oscar entered the cabin and demanded Sam close the flap as he had with me. Nothing happened. He repeated the process, tweaking minor details. Nothing happened. He grabbed my wrist and pulled, attempting to force me inside to show him where I landed when I fell.

"Are you fucking insane? I could have died in there!"

Oscar released me and stood in the low light of the cabin, his fists like bricks resting against his thighs. Sam, hands loosely knotted at the small of his back, stepped between us.

"It doesn't work that way," he giggled, chin ruddy with dried blood. "You can't *force* Nahanni to do what you want it to. Don't ever think you're in control."

Eventually, Oscar gave up. He exited the cabin and wordlessly retraced his steps.

*crunch crunch crunch*

Oscar was walking away. I eased out of my sleeping bag and pressed my eye to the gap in the tent door's zipper. He was not by the coals. A flash of color among the pines gave him away. He braced himself against a tree, his head bent as if inspecting his shoes. Then, as if his legs had been severed at the knees, he disappeared.

*What are you doing?*

I unzipped the tent flap and followed my brother's boot prints. A steady stream of static hissed from Gillian's tent. There was another sound, unsteady, coming from the trees. I pictured a cat without knowing why.

His spine spasmed, arching and collapsing, followed by squelching, like a shoe caught in muck. Oscar shook, a tremor passing from head to feet. The sweat had soaked into his jeans, the top half a darker blue than the bottom. Half a minute passed, and Oscar eased into a sitting position, turning so that I saw him in profile. He held an open can of beans beneath his chin, my dinner from the night before.

His eyes went wild, mouth opening so wide I thought he was going to swallow the can. Instead, he vomited... nothing. His face trembled, stomach undulating. Another silent scream. He dabbed his eyes and wiped his dry mouth. After a minute, he wedged the can into the soil at the base of the tree and swept detritus over it. I hurried back to the tent, leaving the gap in the zipper as I'd found it. Oscar rejoined me after a couple of minutes.

He fell asleep ten minutes later. I knew it by his breaths.

I was prepared to tell him I had to pee, but he didn't wake as I crawled to the flap and unzipped it.

I retraced his steps and located the can beneath a small hill of leaves and pine needles. Inside, a few stray beans, speckled with dirt, clung to its sides. There was nothing else. The can was empty.

I returned it to the base of the tree and shoveled dirt and pine needles over it.

*Oscar, what are you hiding?*

*Son,*

*Hey, I remembered your birthday! Hope this makes up for Christmas! Let me know what you think of the gift. I wasn't sure what to get you, so I had the guy at the store help me. He said it was perfect for a kid your age. Hope you love it!*

*I'm pretty settled in D.C. Korea helped me get used to public transportation, so that's been helpful. There are a lot of museums and memorials. I'm not sure if that's your thing or not, but we can add it to the list. A bit outside of the city there are theme parks. Those are at the top of the list!*

*About your visit, we're going to have to negotiate the amount of time. I know we planned for the whole summer, but I need to use some of my leave to visit Kendra. I'm not sure if I've mentioned her to you before. We dated back in high school and reconnected about a year ago. I'd love it if your mom took me back, but it doesn't look like that's going to happen, and I need to think about my future.*

*For your visit, I'm thinking two weeks. I know it's not what we planned, but it's what I need right now. They're going to be the funnest two weeks of your life, son! Then you get the whole summer with your mom and Oscar.*

*Love,*
*Dad*

# CHAPTER SIX

The clouds were like strips of gauze pinned to the sky. The Valley was still. Branches trembled not from a breeze but the movement of birds and insects, scurrying squirrels digesting the last of their winter stores. Yesterday's chill left with the formless gray canopy. Ten minutes into our walk, I removed my coat and stuffed it into my backpack. Oscar was sweating as well. He had not stopped sweating.

Few words were exchanged before we departed camp. Sam popped out from behind a tree and Oscar demanded he lead us back to the cabin. He refused breakfast, and instead stood at the head of the trail that would take us to the Valley floor. He said nothing while Gillian and I picked at the freeze-dried eggs she prepared, eating in preparation for the day's exertion rather than hunger. I did not tell her about Oscar's early morning sojourn as I did not understand it. It was not dry heaving. It was something else. Oscar *thought* he was vomiting. He would not have hidden an empty can.

"Like I said, the cabin isn't always there. It's not really predictable, either. But I've got some other things to show you," Sam said, mostly directed at Oscar, who grunted and hiked his backpack higher on his shoulders.

As with the day prior, Sam and Oscar pulled ahead. There was no joyful chatter, no gesticulating. My sense of wonder at distant, snow-capped peaks, granite skyscrapers, and a kaleidoscope of petals hoping to catch the eye of an arctic bumblebee faltered. The silence was not meditative but a prelude, a sharp inhalation before the world changed.

Despite his shorter legs, Oscar established a near galloping pace. Sam, wearing the same shirt and seeming more waif-like than when he left our camp the previous evening, stumbled trying to keep up. I was glad Gillian was with me, in body if not in mind. She kept a buffer of several feet between us, slowing when I did to preserve the distance. The baby monitor alternated between static and silence as she triggered the talk function and whispered. What she said and who she thought was on the other end were not known to me. But I had an idea.

I was powerless to make a different choice, to not follow my feet. Not for the first time. My marriage to Cheryl was a mistake I understood in my soul before I knew it in my mind. Like the movies where a character is being chased by a car. Instead of darting left or right, he goes forward hoping, somehow, he can outrun the inevitable. It was the same following the boot prints Oscar stomped into the grass.

We reached the tributary in half the time as the day prior. Oscar hopped across the stone in the stream like an automaton, legs stiff as tree stumps. Sam slipped off it, his legs disappearing into water to the knees. With some effort, he pulled himself upright and shook his legs like a dog.

"Careful, friend. You'll catch your death in water that cold," Sam said before leaping to the shore.

There was blood on his bottom lip he did not seem to notice. When I reached the stone, I discovered its source. The tooth could have been a pebble, an oddly shaped fleck of rock. A speck of crimson gave it away. I pinched it between thumb and forefinger and held it in front of my nose. It did not feel like bone but wax. I squeezed and its shape changed like clay. I rolled my fingers and it smeared between them.

I showed the gritty residue to Gillian, and she smiled not understanding. Had I jumped into the water she would have followed suit. She was walking through a dream, her consciousness gripped by the voice she heard amid static. Sam and Oscar were already gone.

I was alone at the top of the world. In my pocket was the letter that led me there. I chased his words across a continent, and I knew why. Deep down, I knew why. Gillian was right. Everything came back to him.

***

"This isn't the fucking place," Oscar growled.

He paced in a circle, hands on hips, jaw pulsing.

"It is, sorry to say. You just never know with this place. A disappearin' cabin is pretty tame with what else I seen. You gotta trust your senses, though. If you go down the road of not believing what's in front of you, well, that road will drive you straight off a cliff. And if you fall...you might not ever stop."

"What does that mean?" I asked, tired of the riddles.

Sam left Oscar to his pacing and joined me on a boulder hardly big enough for one.

He leaned in and whispered, "If anyone should've figured it out by now it's you."

I almost asked why, but the answer was obvious. I had spoken it to myself only minutes before. I was alone. Oscar's thoughts were corrupted by some idea tied to the cabin, and Gillian was still dreaming. I was alone and off the map. This was the same place as the day before and there was no cabin. It disappeared just as Sam predicted.

"Oscar...what are you doing?" I said, showing my palms as if surrendering.

He held the knife to his side, blade up. His eyes were threaded with bright red capillaries, the brown irises suspended in a net.

"There's no need for that, friend. The Valley's just...takin' a breath," Sam said. "There's lots more to see. Lots more than some ol' cabin."

Sam stood and approached my brother, hands up as if to warm them by a fire.

"It's okay. You're okay. I'm here with you," I said.

Oscar's countenance softened. He blinked a few times, glanced at the knife with a furrowed brow.

"Oscar?" I said.

He looked at me, confused for a moment.

"I...I wanted to kill him. I wanted to cut his fucking throat. Why didn't it happen for me?"

Him. His father.

Everything came back to him.

He returned the knife to its sheath and a shuddering breath rippled through his body. When he looked up it was a face I recognized.

\*\*\*

Oscar's appetite returned, and Sam entertained him with stories of Nahanni as he ate. Gillian beckoned with a head nod.

"How is he?" she asked.

There was no static for the moment.

"Uh, seems like he's coming around. About this, at least. There's other stuff going on with him I'm not sure about."

As I spoke, Gillian pivoted, inches at a time, and I mirrored her movements without realizing it. Our backs were to Oscar and Sam, lost in stories about giants. She began to unbutton her flannel shirt from the bottom. Her concern was a ruse.

"Gill-"

"Shhhhh..."

She stopped at the third button, then parted the fabric.

"Look," she said.

"Look? At what?"

"Look."

She took a single step backward and the sun shone on her belly. A freckle above and to the left of her naval. I remembered it well.

"What am I..."

In full sun the shape of her belly was lost. Noticing my squinting, she inched forward into the shade of a pine tree.

I swallowed, glanced behind to see Oscar nodding as Sam regaled him with some new bit of lore. We were both middle-aged, soft in places that used to be firm, though neither of us were ever athletes. That's not what she was showing me. She framed her belly with her hands, thumbs rising at its center.

"Are you..." I began, then shook my head not wanting to plant the idea if it wasn't true. "What are you showing me?"

She laced her fingers and sighed, "I wasn't. But I am. Somehow. You remember, don't you Joe? You remember what it was like?"

I hid the picture in a book I hoped Cheryl would never open. Gillian's hands within mine forming a heart over her belly. It was hot that day and we were both sweaty. Our enthusiasm waned as the photographer suggested poses that were decidedly *not us*. I liked that picture, though, enough to keep it through a decade of marriage knowing if it was ever found it would be the beginning of the end.

*What if he had been-*

"Let's go!" Oscar shouted, slicing through my thoughts.

Gillian held my gaze for a moment, searching for understanding. I couldn't give it to her. The Valley was supernatural. I believed that much. But this...

"Where to?" I said, stepping around her.

"To the giants!" Oscar said.

\*\*\*

With the sun directly overhead, it was impossible to determine our direction. Once again, we put full faith in Sam, who clarified there were no giants. We would be visiting what he believed was their former refuge. One of many, he assumed, but the only he'd found.

"Does this *disappear* too?" I asked.

"Ha! Not likely, friend! But it might grow legs," he said, then winked.

I winked back, "How's the tooth?"

His eyes flitted from Oscar to Gillian before settling on me.

"Oh, I'm just comin' apart at the seams, huh? My mama used to..."

Sam stopped and began to blink as if facing a strong wind.

"Sam?" Oscar said.

He blinked in one second intervals, lips pulling his mouth into strange shapes. I glimpsed the gap in his teeth, a splotch of crimson amid the pink of his gums. Oscar squeezed his shoulder and gave him a gentle shake. Sam's head tilted back, but he did not respond otherwise.

"Sam?" Oscar said, then waved his arms.

I took a turn, shaking and calling to him, snapping my fingers in front of his face. I studied him, closely, for the first time. The whiskers from cheek to jaw reminded me of roach antennae. They were spaced out evenly, and not densely, as if to give the illusion of a beard. The blinking slowed and he focused on me.

"Sam? What was that? Where did you go?"

He looked away and shook his head, "I, uh, couldn't remember."

"Remember what?" I asked.

"Her. Anything. I couldn't remember anything. I don't know where I..." he began, then scanned the trees, the stream like a strip of molten silver in the distance. His smile formed slowly, unevenly, higher on the left side than the right. "We should get going."

He slid through the group, leaving Oscar, Gillian, and I to decide if we would follow him.

"What happened?" Gillian mouthed.

Sam trudged up an incline moving slower than yesterday, as if he'd aged twenty years overnight. He pressed his thighs as he walked, neck bent so that only his shoulders were visible.

*Headless...*

"I don't know. Seemed like he just spaced for a bit," I said.

"Are we gonna follow him?"

"This couldn't have been his plan. *We* couldn't have been his plan. I don't know how he got here. The story doesn't add up, but, putting that aside, why has he attached himself to us? Doesn't he have his own plan?" I said.

We looked to Oscar. The Valley was his idea.

"I don't know. Some people get off on being the expert. Like when you go to a new city and some bar guy wants to show you all his spots. We could go back to camp. We could wait it out there. Wait for Pilot Bob, I mean. We don't have to keep doing this."

Sam was too far away to have heard, but stopped and turned, "Got somethin' to show you before the giants. You're gonna want a picture of this."

We passed a shrug among our group before Oscar said, "We came this far."

*Giants*, a carrot dangled in front of our faces. Everything Sam told us about the Valley had been true, so why would this be different? We followed, the stream a constant companion to our left, sometimes curling out of sight before reappearing a quarter mile later. There was music in the air, birds twittering at the sun, the thrum of an unseen waterfall. Each breath cleared my head. Questions about Sam were replaced by the brightness of the day, the colors of a meadow connecting one copse of trees to another.

Oscar walked with me, only pulling ahead when the path was too narrow. We talked about Mom, about our childhoods. He did not mention his father but left room for me to speak of mine. My experience in the cabin felt like a dream, the hours in darkness consolidated to a moment.

"Do you remember the sandwiches?" I asked.

"Yep. Two for you and one for me. I had to do it or you wouldn't eat and I would get blamed."

"You weren't just being a good big brother?"

"Come on, Bro. I can be a good big brother and look out for my own ass. Plus, you were kinda pathetic."

"I think it's the saddest thing I've ever heard. Little Joe with his chin on the windowsill waiting for his dad. Isn't it sad?" Gillian said.

Oscar shrugged, "I guess. I didn't mind 'cause I got to watch whatever I wanted on TV. Remember how we'd fight over the remote? How you'd put it in your underwear and run away?"

I laughed, "True, but where did I learn that from?"

"Hey, we're talking about you, not me."

Sam appeared in our path, a finger to his lips. He motioned downward, then stooped to demonstrate. He duckwalked toward a wall of reeds. When he reached them, he nodded for us to follow, pointing at a small body of water beyond.

Once gathered, he whispered, "They like to charge. Stay quiet."

He sidestepped and mimed parting the reeds.

*They like to charge?*

I did not know what I was looking for, and the sun reflecting off the water turned everything the same hazy blue. To my left, Gillian gasped and put a hand over her mouth. I followed her gaze but saw only a small grass island in the pool.

*What?* I mouthed.

She pointed to the island. There was another beside it I had not noticed. Then it moved.

Sam's breath tickled my ear, "You probably won't get a better view. They don't come out of the water during the day. Imagine a wooly hippo. That's what they look like. They hibernate like bears but underground."

I wished a stray cloud would pass in front of the sun. It was too bright. Just a hairy hump and two lumps of what might have been ears. A brief geyser near the opposite shore sent a ripple of adrenaline through my body.

"They might have blowholes like whales. Can't see through the hair," Sam whispered, then pointed. "Look."

Across the pond and above the treetops was a granite column maybe two-hundred feet in height. Taller columns stood behind it, fading into a blur in the distance.

"About halfway up. You see it?" Sam said.

"I see something. Is it a...crack in the rock?" I said.

"It's a nest. Sometimes you can see it peaking over the side."

"Eagle?" Oscar asked.

There was a low rumbling from the pond, bubbles boiling on its surface. Sam shook his head and mimed zipping his lips.

Gillian slid out of her backpack, unzipped it enough to reach inside. She withdrew her camera and pulled the lens cap off with a barely audible *click*.

As quiet as a sigh, the *wooly hippos* disappeared.

"Shit!" Gillian seethed.

Sam tapped her on the shoulder, finger to lips again. He motioned for us to follow, one finger in the air until we could no longer see the water.

His voice was just above a whisper, "That was a bull. A big one, and his lady. Probably got a nice little harem in that pond. Got to be quiet not because of him but because of the ones you *don't* see."

"What are they?" Oscar said, his face halfway between fascinated and terrified.

"Ain't my place to name 'em. They look like wooly hippos. That's the best I can manage. Nahanni has a name for 'em, but since I don't know it, I won't speak it," Sam said, then turned and resumed walking. "Though they're usually not this far out."

"Far out from what?" I asked.

Sam didn't answer.

"What about the nest?" I tried. "What builds a nest that big?"

Sam shrugged, "I don't know. Thankfully, I've never seen one up close. I have found feathers longer than my arm."

\*\*\*

The world transitioned, trees becoming leafier, the air thick as soup. When out in the open the sun felt like a heat lamp on the back of my neck. Sweat did not evaporate but coated my skin like cooking oil. It soaked through to my socks, and I was soon out of water. Oscar was shirtless and as slick as an otter.

"This doesn't feel like northern Canada," I gasped.

The march demanded so much energy I absorbed little of my surroundings. I could only stare at my boots, the pattern of exploded sweat droplets on the toes.

"I don't think we're in northern Canada," Gillian said.

Her shirt was tied above the bump of her belly, more prominent now than it had been three hours before.

"What do you mean?" I asked.

"None of what's happening makes sense. The cabin, the monitor," she said, brandishing it like a grenade. "Have you ever heard of a wooly hippo? I don't think there are rules anymore, Joe."

"Then why are we still doing this?"

She glanced at her belly.

"Is it getting bigger?" I asked.

"Yes. And what happens when...what happens if I have to deliver here?"

I could no longer hear Oscar, whose rasping breaths had been easy to follow as I navigated with my head down. Gillian passed the baby monitor to me and then dug into her pocket. The denim was wet with sweat and tight against her skin.

"This is what I was letting go of. What I planned to, anyway."

We traded. A baby monitor for the two by three-inch image of our son. The one from her nightstand.

"And now this is happening," she said, thrusting her belly. "And I don't know what it means. And I know you think I'm crazy. I know I'm the only person who hears him, but I believe you, Joe. I believe you saw your father in that cabin. I believe you were in there for as long as you said. The sooner we accept these things are happening the sooner we will find out why."

The paper was no longer glossy. Its edges were rounded from handling. I turned it over.

*Joseph*

My heart raced.

"What other name could I give him?"

"I..."

There was nothing to be said. My life went on after Gillian. I loved again, even if it wasn't the right love. I had a career and traveled. Those hours in the delivery room, our ears tortured by a thousand sounds reminding us of our failure...I walled myself off from them and kept living. I never mourned my son.

My son.

"Hang onto it if you like. I might ask for it back, though."

Gillian walked away with the baby monitor in front of her face.

"...knows your name now..."

\*\*\*

"There's a lot of caves in Nahanni. I've explored dozens, but this is one is special," Sam said, hands on his hips as if he had built it himself.

I didn't care about giants. More than anything, I wanted to sit in the shade and drink cold water. I could not fathom the trek back to the camp.

"Come on. It's just inside."

Sunlight spilled about fifty feet into the cave. After another fifty feet the shadows darkened to blackness. It was October cool there, the change in temperature so abrupt I was soon shivering while still glossy with sweat.

"So, what are we looking for? A big bone or something? A war drum?" Oscar asked.

"Not quite. Not the best light for it, but look up," Sam said, pointing at the wall to our right.

The images were flaked and faded, the artistry challenged by the rough surface.

"Not stuff you'll recognize mostly. Those animals might have been from a million years ago. Or, could just be a part of Nahanni I haven't been to. It's a big place. Bigger than it looks on a map."

Gillian retrieved her camera again. She snapped a picture, adjusted the zoom, and took another.

"How do you know it was giants? There were other tribes here, right? The Dene?" Oscar asked.

Sam shuffled a few feet to the left, eyes scanning back and forth.

"There!" he said, his voice echoing into the bowels of the cave like a gunshot. "The wooly hippo is about the size of a car. Do you see that?"

It was a crude rendering, the color blending into the ruddy brown of the cave wall. I could make out the borders, and it was roughly the shape of a hippopotamus as Sam suggested.

"What's wrong with the head?" Gillian asked.

"That's not its head. That's a boulder," Sam said, then demonstrated picking up a rock and smashing it.

"You mean they, the giants, killed them by dropping boulders on their heads?" Oscar said.

"That's what I mean."

"How do you know they're not just stories?" I asked.

"I don't know. I believe they're not stories because of everything else I've seen here," Sam said, then rubbed his hands together. "And the best part is, we're still on the outskirts."

"Of what?" I asked.

"Of the *real* Nahanni. You've seen some of the stuff that leaked out. I'll take you tomorrow. If you wanna go."

Before we could answer, Sam coughed. Once, twice. A third time and something landed on the cave floor, wet like a spoonful of yogurt. He stepped on it and smeared it with his shoe.

"A bug," he said, lips bright with blood. "I...we should head back. I'll still take you tomorrow."

He nearly sprinted out of the cave, not waiting for a response. Oscar followed but Gillian hovered near me. Most of the images were too faded or foreign. One I initially thought was a blemish caught my eye. It was black, ovular in shape but flat across the bottom, and dotted with pinpricks of white. The night sky, maybe. Perhaps a constellation that was meaningful for them.

"Look, Joe," Gillian said, pointing.

Whatever Sam expelled was no longer there. The cave floor was not even wet.

*Son,*

*Sorry we haven't had as much time together these last few years. Retirement is like starting all over. New job and a new home. Lots of little things that get in the way. I haven't followed through with much for you. I hope you know I do care. Sometimes caring is just something you hold in your heart. You might not have proof of it even if it's there.*

*Love,*
*Dad*

# CHAPTER SEVEN

I woke to what I thought was a bear growling. Something big. From what I had seen yesterday, a bear was the best I could hope for. I clawed my way out of the tent and left a pile of nightmares on the wadded shirt that served as my pillow.

The scene upon exiting the tent was confusing. Gillian stood to my right, her left arm cradling the underside of her pregnant belly. Her right hand touched her cheek as she looked with concern at Oscar, who hunched over the ashes of the campfire. The sound came from him. The animal noises. He retched, stood to his full height, and wiped his lips. Then he bent over, hands on knees, and retched again.

He produced nothing, only the sound. In between expulsions he mumbled. *Sorry* I think he said, as he looked from me to Gillian.

Sam, unconcerned, sat with his back against a tree trunk. Did he even return to his camp the night before? I tried to remember, but time ran together. Pilot Bob had advised me to keep track of the days. What day was it?

"Oscar, are you okay?" I asked after it seemed the sickness had passed.

He dabbed at his mouth, cheeks streaked with tears.

"It's this fucking place," he said, then turned and jabbed a finger as sharp as a dart at Sam. "You know what's happening. Don't tell me you don't! I've been clean for years!"

Sam took his time responding. He appeared unbothered by what he witnessed and unaffected by the anger underlying Oscar's accusation. He stood, dusted his hands off on his pants and said, "And what do you think is happening?"

Oscar's face relaxed, arms slack at his sides. He stood a couple of inches shorter than Sam but was twice his size. His fingers spider-walked and came to a rest on the hilt of his knife.

"Oscar!" I shouted.

He abandoned the knife and reached a hand up, a thumb in the hollow of Sam's left cheek and four fingers on the opposite side. Oscar squeezed for just a second.

"The fuck?" he said, stumbling backwards. From where I stood, I saw the side of Sam's face before he hid it in the crook of his elbow. The impression of Oscar's thumb was visible in the skin, as if his face was made of dough. It was a glimpse in shadowed light, and my attention was quickly diverted.

Oscar backpedaled and sputtered like a failing engine. His eyes swelled like toad bellies as he mumbled about *sobriety*, then looked at the ashes with something akin to embarrassment.

"Oscar, there's nothing there. You're not actually sick," I said.

I kneeled, scooped a handful of ashes and sprinkled them over the ground.

"Are you seeing something different?" I asked.

Oscar only blinked.

Behind us, Gillian seethed, her right hand now atop her belly.

"He's kicking," she said, mouth quivering as if restraining a smile. "Do you want to fee-"

"We've got a long way to go yet, and I'm not feelin' so good," Sam said, smiling wide enough to show more of his teeth had fallen out. "Also, you're gonna need to pack your things. We'll set up camp in the *real* Nahanni. If you're still up for it."

Gillian turned away, cradling her belly with both arms. Sam stared at me as he massaged his cheeks, patting and smoothing the skin.

"You know more than you're letting on," I said. "What is the *real* Nahanni? What are we getting ourselves into?"

Sam could have been a disappointed father handed a report card with all Ds. He crossed his arms over his chest. As he alluded to the day before, he expected me to understand better than Oscar and Gillian.

"Well, you'll get an answer to that question. Answers to other questions you haven't even thought of yet. I don't know all the answers, though, and just 'cause I *know* it don't mean it's t*rue*. I'm walkin', with or without you. I'll give you a few minutes to gather your things and then I'm goin'."

We interpreted his statement as an order and disassembled the tents with little conversation. At Sam's suggestion, we left the heavier food items in a bag hung from a tree branch. He said we would need to be light on our feet. *Quick.* I wasn't sure if we were coming back. I wasn't sure if I would see Pilot Bob again. It felt like we had been in the Valley for more than a week. The sun never truly setting, the seconds that passed as hours in the cabin. I counted time by the number of meals I had eaten, and those were beginning to run together. Maybe Bob had already come and gone.

That day I did not feel like Bilbo Baggins on an adventure. I felt like Frodo gazing over the black gate of Mordor. We entered the Valley as we had the previous days. Instead of following the path that would take us to the cabin site we walked the opposite direction, passing by the log Oscar and I shared the first day. It seemed like so long ago. It was sunny, still, a bit warmer but not warm.

"This doesn't have to be somber," Sam said. "Yeah, I didn't tell you everything I know about this place, but I couldn't have done that, could I? You wouldn't have believed me. Now, I think you will."

We walked through a meadow that felt like magic the first day. It was still beautiful, but I was detached from it. As if it was a movie set. Within an hour we reached the area we'd encountered the wall of fog. I think so, anyway. Instead of fog there was a smooth, still lake. Gillian could have walked into it without knowing, but I don't think she was meant to. It was beautiful in that same detached way. I wondered if there were monsters lurking beneath its surface.

This time, Sam was in front by several paces. Our group stayed clustered together, Oscar at the tip of our triangle. Maybe it was an instinct to protect ourselves from whatever was happening to Sam. He moved quickly, but his stride was uncoordinated, as if his limbs were numbing in random places. A little past the lake, Sam stopped. So did we to maintain the buffer between us. He turned and beckoned as he did with the wooly hippo. Although he didn't smile there was a lightness in his eyes, a spark of curiosity. We joined him and discovered its source.

There was a Dall Sheep, a ram, black as a shadow.

"Aren't those usually white?" Oscar asked.

"They're *always* white," Sam clarified. "But that's not what's interesting. Look closer."

I thought there was a clump of grass drooping from its mouth. Its jaw worked like a cow chewing cud, but the color was wrong. It was too pale. Off to the side, almost completely hidden by knee-high grass and flowers, I noticed the jutting horns of a fallen ram. There was a strip of red from its neck to the middle of its spine, a gouge. The black ram watched us, its posture confident. It chewed the flesh with teeth not suited to the task and stared.

"Those aren't carnivores," Gillian said.

"No, they're not," Sam confirmed.

"So why would it do that?" she asked.

"Well, just because it's dead don't mean he killed it. Could've died of natural causes and...that's a lot of protein to go to waste. Or coulda been a dominance thing. When those rams knock horns, you can hear it from a mile away. Land a hard enough blow and it can kill instantly. Let's move on."

We stopped about once an hour, to nibble or fill our water bottles. We said little, each of us processing our circumstances privately. The color returned to Oscar's cheeks, and he ate as if he did not expect to vomit the food minutes later. The path led us into a passageway of sorts, with a sloping rock wall to our left, what I guessed was west, and shear granite to our right. The land beyond did not feel different, but like a continuation of the previous half dozen or so miles of terrain.

My right ankle screamed at the earth beneath my boot. Soft soil recently thawed from its winter stasis. My bones were broken glass, the old injury resurrected. It made my last few years of service in the military challenging, but I was determined to retire on my own terms, not because the Air Force made me. Gillian was six months pregnant or appeared to be, and her pace had not slowed. I said nothing of the pain but tried to match her gait.

When Oscar signaled he was ready for a break and a more substantial meal, I unloaded where I stood, sitting on my backpack and taking the weight off my feet. He was not privy to the conversations I had with Gillian about the obvious change to her body.

"You weren't pregnant when you got here, right?" Oscar asked, spraying granola.

"I wasn't. Wouldn't have been possible."

Oscar nodded, "And the baby monitor?"

She patted her backpack, "It's in here. Just needed some time with my own thoughts, I guess."

"And what have you decided?"

Although Oscar asked the question, Gillian looked at me when she replied, "That I don't know anything. None of us do. We're sitting here like this is normal, like somehow in a few days we're going to be back home living our lives. I don't think that's going to happen. There is no *normal* after this. And we might not make it home."

During the periods of silence, I watched Sam, content then to be separated from us. His attention alternated between the sun and his hands.

"Can you tell us now?" I asked.

"Tell you what?" he responded in a flat tone.

"Something? Anything? Give us a reason not to turn around."

He arched an eyebrow at me and smirked as if to imply that was not an option and I knew it.

"Ask me a question."

Oscar and Gillian were still wrestling with the idea she proposed, that we might be marching toward our deaths.

"What is Nahanni doing to us?" I asked.

"I don't know," he said.

"You don't know?"

He shook his head, "Ask another question."

I threw my hands up, "Where are you taking us? And don't say *the real Nahanni* if you're not going to explain what that means."

He sat up a little taller, spat a tooth into his hand, showed it to me. Then he mashed it between his fingers. This time there was no blood.

"That's a tough question but a fair one. I'll do my best to answer. Just know there are limits to my knowledge, which'll make sense later. Nahanni is...*haunted*. Now, there are a lot of layers to that word, but it's the best one I can think of. It isn't haunted in the sense there are ghosts around, though there might be. I just mean to say I've never seen one before.

"Now, in every haunted house story, there's some origin, some source. Sometimes it's in the basement. Sometimes the attic. That's where the bad thing happened. Same is true for Nahanni, but it's not a bad thing that happened. I don't think so. That's another limit to what I know."

I interrupted, "What is it here?"

He frowned, "That's gonna have to wait a bit. But I promise you'll see it. In the spooky stories, the attic or the basement is where the bad thing is concentrated. The haunting radiates from it. Make sense? You might have a ghostie in the living room, but its skeleton is under the floor."

Reading my confusion, he said, "I'm doin' a terrible job of explaining this, but there is a Heart to Nahanni. Everything you've seen and everything you haven't seen...that comes from the Heart."

"Is that where you're taking us to?" Gillian asked.

Sam sighed. He began to tug at his finger. I thought he was trying to pop the joint, but he pulled harder, and harder. His lips rolled into a thin line. I imagined his teeth grinding into paste, him spitting it at me. Eventually, there was a *THWOCK* and his arm, from the elbow, popped free of his shirt sleeve. The hand and forearm were now disconnected from the rest of the arm.

Gillian screamed.

Oscar cried out as if shot and crawled away, throwing his protein bar as if it was a rattlesnake.

Sam turned the arm over, inspecting the bloodless wound like a kid deciding whether a rock was worth keeping. I couldn't focus on it. I knew what it was supposed to look like, the bone and muscle, the tendons and veins. I saw it, in flashes, or maybe a memory from before. I patted my hip, searching for a kit that wasn't there, and the tourniquet within.

He pulled his arm off. He pulled his own fucking arm off like popping a dryer ball out of a shirt sleeve. Like how his teeth kept falling out of his mouth.

He dropped the arm on the grass and said, "That was really starting to itch. Now, I bet you have another question."

Before I could ask, he stood, which required more effort considering the loss of half of his left arm.

"Tell you what, we'll walk and talk. I don't know how much time I have, and we've got miles to go."

Gillian slapped a hand on her belly. She looked in the direction we'd come from, probably considering a return to the camp. Although, there was no camp to return to. For a time, Oscar stared at the arm, unblinking, not understanding. There was no understanding, this or much of what we witnessed in Nahanni.

"What the fuck? What the fuck?" Oscar muttered. "The longer I stare the less I see it."

He scratched his sides and shook his head.

"It's...disappearing," Gillian said.

Sam slowly walked away from the group, true to his declaration that he would leave with or without us.

"Oscar, what are we going to do?"

He was my big brother, after all, and a natural problem solver. Oscar crawled to the arm and tapped the half-curled fist as if fearing it might explode. That wonder we felt witnessing the evidence of giants, or the tufted ears of the wooly hippo, was gone. In its place was a sort of fascination tinged with dread. Oscar needed it to make sense. He could not achieve this in his mind. He was far too tactile for that.

After determining the severed arm was not a bomb, he nodded at Sam.

"I think she's right," he said. "About us not making it home. I don't know if that's true or not, but I think if we head that way. Like we're going back camp, it might just lead us back here."

That made sense in a way I could not explain.

"Gillian?" I said. She was trapped between wanting to protect her baby, the baby that should not have been, and the need for answers to a private question. There were layers to her calculus not apparent to me then. Outside of that, it could have been the simple fear of walking alone.

"Yeah. Okay," she said.

We gathered around the arm.

"I think if we looked away it wouldn't be there," Oscar said.

"What about him? Where is he when we're not looking at him?" I asked.

\*\*\*

Sam's pace was slow, which might have been a result of his deteriorated state rather than grace he extended to give us time. We caught up to him after a minute of brisk walking. He did not give us the answers. Did not suggest questions to ask. We traversed the lumpy terrain, and my mind was incapable of forming new thoughts. Instead, there was a five-second loop of Sam tugging his finger and the forearm sliding free of his sleeve.

Not including Gillian, everything that happened I had an explanation for. Teeth fall out. Maybe there was a secret population of wooly hippos. Undiscovered species exist outside of human observation. If such an animal did exist, it made sense that it would be in Nahanni. The wall of fog was just fog, even if its structure was unprecedented. My experience in the cabin could have been a hallucination. Could I believe my interpretation of time filtered through a dream state? As for Gillian, I hadn't decided. But I thought, at the root of it, was her need to have had our son, to have become a mother.

The environment shifted around me. The evergreens were replaced by deciduous trees, their leaves glossy from a recent rain. There were sounds, too. Maybe already present for a while and I just hadn't noticed them. In the narrow meadow between bands of forest, jungle more precisely, we walked as the calls of unseen birds volleyed over our heads. If we were in the same place we landed days ago, geographically, I should have seen granite towers, snow-capped peaks. Although we walked many miles, those landmarks would have been visible for many more.

We didn't ask the question. Sam just started talking.

"I don't think I'm real," he said. His voice was tentative, wounded, as if he'd only just discovered this fact.

"What do you mean *not real*?" I asked.

He kept walking, his gait awkward and uncoordinated.

"I can't explain it as well as I'd like. I think I *was* real at some point. I think I haven't been real for a long time. I don't know. It's like I was asleep. Asleep and not dreaming for...I don't know how long, then I woke up on that ledge. Can I ask you a question?"

"Of course," I said.

"What year is it?"

When I told him he stopped and nodded. He turned to me with a placeholder smile and said, "That's about a sixty-year difference from the last thing I remember. I kinda knew not to talk about it. I knew it wasn't something I wanted to hear."

"So, you were gone and something brought you back?" I said.

"Yes," he said. "But not all the way."

"What was it?"

Sam motioned for Oscar and Gillian to join us. He pointed to his throat and shook his head. His voice had lost resonance with each step.

"I'm not gonna make it there, but I'll do my best to explain it."

"Explain what?" Gillian asked.

"It. The Heart of Nahanni."

We walked at Sam's pace.

"The Heart of Nahanni is...a *chaos engine*. I think that's a term from before."

"From before?" I said.

"From before whatever happened. In that space where I was not awake and not dreaming. What you see in our world isn't by accident. Although it kinda is. The Heart introduces *chance*. I don't remember much from before. Just bits and pieces. Kinda like that adage about blind men touching an elephant. I remember some of it, but mostly I remember what the Heart wants me to. You'll forgive me if I stumble through this. It's not easy to explain and I might not be right about it."

"Take your time," Gillian said.

"I plan on it," Sam said with a smile. "I think I came here a long time ago. *Time* is a funny word, but we'll use it as it's intended and as you understand it. Maybe I came for the same reason you did. I can't say. I just know there was a before, then there was the Heart, and there is now. By introducing chance I mean...it's like those science experiments. A thousand attempts but it was the thousand and first that worked. So, things enter the chaos engine and go..." Sam made a motion with his fingers demonstrating he did not know where. "And something else comes through. An exchange maybe? This world and another? This reality and another or time and another? Just like those experiments, one thousand exchanges might change nothing. But the thousand and first...it could change everything."

"I'm not sure I'm following," Gillian said.

"I don't expect you to. It'll make more sense when you get there. I entered the chaos engine something like sixty years ago in your time. I'm not sure what happened after that."

Each of us digested the information in our own way, mostly in silence. When presented with something completely alien to a lived experience, the mind blanks. I imagine it's similar for people who believe they've encountered the supernatural, ghosts or Sasquatch. Something wholly unique.

Mom used to buy connect-the-dots coloring books from the dollar bin. The quality wasn't the greatest, but I loved them because she was trying. That dollar could have been something for herself. Instead, it was a pouch of chewing gum for Oscar and connect-the-dots for me. Sometimes the picture didn't make sense even after the lines were drawn. My brain misfired with Sam's information. I saw the dots, but there were no numbers guiding me.

Sam's language regarding the chaos engine, the *Heart* of Nahanni, generated an image of random steampunk machinery, pipes and gears, panels with frosted windows and brass knobs. It was the best I could manage.

Thirty minutes passed before I reassessed myself and my surroundings. The trees around me were reminiscent of my childhood dinosaur books, tall with broad leaves shining brightly in a sun I could not detect. There were new sounds too. Chirps and chitters, wails of warning at the sight of four predators, though one was clearly wounded. I searched for the source, the volume suggesting the animals responsible were near, likely within one hundred feet. Though the leaves fidgeted the animals remained hidden.

"I remember them from before," Sam said, his voice husky.

"What do they look like?" Oscar asked.

Sam shrugged, "Only seen the eyes at night. Yellow. Taller than you'd think by the sound. Think it was just my fire that kept 'em away."

To that point in Nahanni, the insects we encountered were of the pollen-collecting variety. We were told the biting flies and mosquitos that plagued much of the Arctic and sub-Arctic were not as prevalent in the Valley. I began to make peace with Gillian's assertion that we were no longer *in* Nahanni. Although insects were not my only evidence of this, they were certainly the most persistent. Mosquitos the size of my palm lancing through the fabric of my shirt, the needle-sharp proboscis stabbing skin in areas of my body that were difficult to access. An unspoken arrangement formed. One among us would point to an area he or she could not reach and the nearest person to it would smack it, the mosquito, or whatever it was, exploding its gray innards often tinged with red from its most recent meal.

Sam's pace slowed to a halting shuffle. He covered as much distance swaying to his left and right as he did moving forward. Finally, he stopped, bent over at the waist, head shaking like Oscar after expelling ghost vomit.

"Are you okay?" I asked, a stupid question but my life had not prepared me for this moment. My hand hovered over his back without touching it.

"No," he whispered, and instead of standing took a knee. "You're going to have to leave me."

A tremor of panic sparked from my chest and caught fire in my veins. Although my faith in Sam's intentions wavered during our short time together, without him we were truly lost.

"Just keep walking in the direction you're headed. Stay away from the trees and you'll get there. I don't doubt you could do it with your eyes closed," he said, then chuckled. "It's been calling to you from the beginning."

"The Heart?" Oscar said.

He nodded, "In its way..." he trailed off then lifted the stub of his arm. "It doesn't hurt if you're worried about that."

"What do we do when we get there?" I asked.

"You'll know when you get there. That isn't for me to decide. It might not be the Heart that decides it."

"It's not right to leave you," I said.

Sam flashed corpse-colored gums, "You need to redefine the *you* part of that thought. There is no *you* meaning *me*."

I couldn't help but remember Sam's previous directive, to not disbelieve our own eyes. He was still before me, very real though not very normal.

"Would you mind?" Sam said, pointing to his shoe.

"Mind?"

"Taking it off. I can't really manage now."

I kneeled, the weight of by backpack nearly toppling me, then untied the knot in the laces.

"Pull it? If you don't mind," Sam said.

I grabbed it at the heel and felt the canvas material collapse as I squeezed and tugged. The shoe came off and the sock lay on the grass like a deflated balloon.

"I thought so," Sam said.

It didn't feel right, regardless of what he was. Maybe if we brought him to the Heart he would find his answers. I looked to Oscar for guidance. Between the two of us he was the better at making difficult decisions. But his gaze was fixed on the tree line. Sweat dappled his upper lip and his fingers were curled into tight fists. I'm not sure where he was, but it wasn't with me in that moment. I pivoted to Gillian and found that reality repeated. The baby monitor rested atop her belly, the static that had become background noise since its discovery rose above the din of hooting and bird songs. This was my decision now.

I kneeled beside Sam again, placed a hand on his shoulder. My fingers sank, as if beneath the fabric was soft mud. His voice was not a whisper, but it was obvious the anatomy of his throat had changed. What came out sounded like a warped vinyl record played at the wrong speed.

"You still haven't figured it out yet, have you?"

Despite the strained texture of his voice, the annoyance, the anger was evident.

"Figured what out?" I said to the crown of his head.

He sighed and lifted the flap of his arm, looked at it, and returned it to his side.

"Isn't it interesting...that they're just what you thought they were."

They? Oscar and Gillian? What did I think they were?

He nodded at Oscar, "A junkie. Just like you knew he was."

"I don't-"

"And she," he said, nodding at Gillian. "Just can't get herself right, huh? She's so infatuated with you, huh? Look at her. Exactly what you thought she was. Pathetic. Or is it? Have you decided yet?"

"Sam I-"

"Shut up," he gurgled. "You still haven't figured it out. You're the leader of this little gaggle. They both came here for you in some way. Now look at them. Look what you did to them."

"I didn't do this!" I shouted.

Oscar had been sitting on his backpack, hands folded beneath his bowed head. He looked up at the noise then lowered his head again. Gillian held the baby monitor out to the side, her attention bouncing from Sam to me.

"Of course you didn't. Look at me," he said, raising his leg, the sock empty at the end of it. "You didn't do that either."

"How could I?"

"Maybe it could only happen in Nahanni. It's true what I told you. I came to this park a long time ago. Then there was the Heart. Now I am here. What happened between the Heart and now I don't know. I think I left something of myself behind. A residue. An imprint. *Behind* isn't the right word for it. There is no *behind*. There are only different perspectives. It was enough, I guess, for you to cobble together something resembling a person. You don't even realize you're doing it. I understand that."

I did not cobble together a human being. I did not reach across time to imprison his consciousness inside of a conjured body.

"Think of it this way. What will be left when I'm gone?"

"When you're gone?"

He flapped his arm stump.

"I'm disappearing. What will be left when I'm gone? What can you hold?"

There would be nothing. No evidence. Only stories of petroglyphs and a magical cabin, a wooly hippo and a severed arm that might already be gone.

"Nothing. I came from nothing and to nothing I return. Do you know what I did at night when you went to sleep?"

I shook my head.

"I walked a hundred feet away and stood against a tree. Waited for you to wake up. Waited to play my part in whatever this is. I don't know what will happen to me. But I'd rather you not be here to witness it. So, if you could kindly fuck off and leave me be. Now and forever."

\*\*\*

Oscar had not spoken for over an hour. Gillian only did so in whispers. I caught fragments of her conversation but stopped paying attention. From what I had seen, I could not discount the possibility she was communicating, in some way, with our son. I didn't believe that was happening, but it might have been.

For that hour, alone with my thoughts, I could not help but wonder what I would find if I returned to the place we left Sam. A pile of clothes. Maybe a headless corpse. That would be fitting. There was nothing I could hold, nothing he had given me. There was only the information in my mind. But I didn't do it. I couldn't have done it.

The sun set, really set, exciting whatever watched us from the trees.

*BEYOOP! BEYOOP!*

I did not know how much further we needed to travel to reach the Heart of Nahanni. It could have been miles or feet, neither distance an appealing proposition in darkness. My body announced its displeasure, the pain in my ankle cutting through the adrenaline. I could go no further. Sam told us to stay away from the trees. There was only one choice to make. I made it for myself and my companions, walking behind me but wandering inside their own heads.

I stopped and dropped my gear. Gillian followed suit and Oscar walked past me like a river breaking around a boulder. I watched him for five seconds, ten seconds, then finally called out. In the dying light, his shoulders flinched, the sound of his name interrupting the bombardment of howls from either side of us. He kept walking. From behind, I saw his right arm bent at the elbow, fingers once again resting on the hilt of the knife.

I let him go.

As I had in our childhood. As a young man, and many times since then. I let him go.

He was already somewhere else.

My tent was on Oscar's back. Gillian and I set up hers. To do this meant relinquishing the baby monitor, and she seemed to return to herself without the distraction.

"Have you ever seen a sky like that?" she asked when we were done, both hands bracing the back of her hips. Her belly was as full as I could remember from before. Above us, the night sky was not one I recognized, the familiar constellations gone, stars much brighter than any I recalled. There was a blurry, blue-green haze half the size of a full moon. Another planet?

"Do you ever wonder if somewhere in the universe there is a constellation that spells out your name, like, your whole name?" she asked.

The question stirred a flutter of nostalgia that felt like warm soup in my stomach. Cheryl would never have asked it. We didn't have conversations like that. In retrospect, the formative years of my relationship with Gillian were the best of my life. Outside of her I had a tumbleweed for a father, guided by the wind. A mother who jumped into the deep end of life's pool without knowing how to swim. I loved her more than anything, and it was just enough to keep her from drowning. Oscar was...well, Oscar. He was the brother whose eyes were not the same shade as mine. The brother I tried to forget.

I poured all of myself into Cheryl. Maybe that's why I held on for so long. To give all of yourself and it not be enough...

We built a fire. Thankfully, the flint and striker kit was in my backpack, not Oscar's. The *BEYOOPs* grew angry at the sight of the flames.

I changed shirts. The other was crispy with dried sweat. When I emerged from the tent I saw Gillian there, glowing with firelight. Her smile serene, belly unmistakable. There was no thought, no debate. I sat behind her and draped my arms over her shoulders. She leaned into me.

Her pulse beneath my fingers did not quicken. It was like she expected this moment would happen.

"Are you still here with me?" I asked.

She inhaled, held it, passed the breath through pursed lips.

"I never left."

Beyond the flames, among the trees, little yellow lights blinked on and off like paired fireflies hovering.

"What do you think is really happening?"

Another long breath. She laced her fingers within mine, rubbed her cheek against the inside of my forearm.

"I think it's different for each of us. Your brother is...fighting things. You had your own experience. Although it doesn't seem like much has happened since then. And for me, it might be a dream, a shared hallucination. Or it might be a second chance."

It was true. Oscar's apparent withdrawal persisted throughout the journey, and Gillian's metamorphosis was not fleeting like the cabin. Though, neither phenomenon had anything to do with me. What did Nahanni want from me? Maybe it needed me to be stable. For my judgement not to be clouded so I could lead the others. Had Gillian been paying attention to my conversation with Sam?

My eyes ached both from the smoke of the fire and from the weariness of the past few days. But this was a moment I wanted to hold onto. Gillian in my arms. The strange, beautiful sky above with its unnamed stars, the new constellations. But as the fire consumed the wood that fed it, the intensity of the light waned, and the yellow eyes came closer. Down from the trees, crouching in the grass. Silent now.

Sam was right. They were taller than I thought they would be. Or maybe I already knew that.

*Son,*

*Sorry I couldn't make it to your graduation. We had a graduation here and, unfortunately, the dates conflicted. Hope a little cash might smooth things over. I'll be there for college. I promise.*

*Dad*

# CHAPTER EIGHT

I tended the fire for the next several hours as the new stars above me shifted positions in the sky. I had only seen the champagne-colored band of the Milky Way a few times in my life. In Afghanistan and in the west Texas desert. What I saw that night was similar but not the same. It was brighter and narrower, like ten thousand clustered jewels of various sizes and colors.

The yellow-eyed animals waited in the trees and the tall grass for the fire to die down sufficiently. For what ultimate purpose I could only guess. I was unaware of the passage of time, my estimates only a guess. I could not assign a clock number to when it happened, but a ripple of panic passed among the creatures. Panic to my ears, at least. The timber of their *BEYOOP*s spiking with alarm. They retreated into the darkness beyond the fire and fled on some other errand.

Gillian had fallen asleep in my arms. I roused her then, fed the fire, and we crawled into the tent too weary even to unzip the sleeping bag.

\*\*\*

I must have dreamed, but it was chaotic, a mirror of the previous day. I was startled out of sleep and lost any tether to the images in the dreams. I woke to Gillian's face inches from mine, the spray of freckles forming a bridge from one cheek to the other a familiar constellation.

She unbuttoned my jeans and said, "I'll stop if you want me to."

Those were the only words we exchanged.

We fit together perfectly. Though our bodies were different than the last time, that fact was the same. There was no distance between us, like a boat rising and falling but never leaving the water. Underlying her passion was a need bordering on desperation. When she guided me inside the heat of her stole my breath. It was more than that. For a few moments, Gillian on top with her hands on my chest, we were still. Both of us etching this moment into our memories. It was like coming home after years of traveling and finding that your key still worked. Gillian was home.

I surrendered to her that morning in that lush, beautiful land serenaded by birds I could not picture and that no man had ever seen. We finished together, as we almost always did. That was not a surprise. Then I began to weep, and I turned my face away from her. She moved behind, angled her belly so she could embrace me.

"It's okay," she whispered. "I know."

\*\*\*

We didn't pack up the tent, maybe in the belief we were not coming back. We walked, hands knotted, as the lovers we had always been.

Answering my question before I asked, Gillian said, "It's in my backpack, just in case."

"Is it not working anymore?"

"I haven't tried since yesterday. It probably is, but I don't know if I'm talking with him."

I allowed her space to develop her thoughts.

"I think I'm talking to the possibility of him. And this..." she said, making a swirling motion of her belly. "...can't be real. I would have said it was impossible, but yesterday I watched a man pull his own arm off. I don't know, Joe. I'm just going forward now."

"This morning..."

"This morning I made it real. I had to try. No, I didn't use you, Joe. It could only ever be you. And I've wanted to do that since the first day you decided you were okay without me."

Other times we strayed into this territory, dancing around the borders that defined our relationship, I pulled away. But I didn't then. I squeezed her hand tighter.

"How is it you don't hate me?" I asked.

"I can't hate you for not knowing something the way I did. Hating you for that would be hating myself. Not to say I don't. I have hated myself for a lot over the years, but never for loving you."

Our watchers were silent, recovering from last night's disturbance.

*Oscar*

Gillian sensed the jolt that passed through me.

"What is it?"

"Last night. Those things. Those yellow-eyed things. They all left at once. What if they caught up to Oscar?"

There was only one direction he could have gone, if he followed Sam's suggestion to stay away from the trees. Unless Oscar did not abide that directive, we were walking in his footsteps.

"Do you think he was trying to reach it last night? To reach it by himself?" Gillian asked.

"He's got something on his mind I haven't figured out. You've seen the outbursts. The sweating. I do think he is clean, but I'm not sure what that means for him. That he believes he is suffering through withdrawal. It's as real as your belly."

"What about the cabin?"

"The stuff with his dad?"

"Yes."

"When he's detoxing every emotion is magnified. And I can't imagine the anger he must feel for his father. I can't compare it to mine."

I searched for evidence of him as we walked, slowly, my ankle feeling like an overripe tomato in my boot, which bulged from swelling. Gillian demanded I allow her to help me. I draped an arm across her shoulders, and we hobbled together one step at a time. Maybe this obvious sign of weakness was what they were waiting for. The trees had been still, silent that morning, only an occasional bird call from somewhere far away. The wind carved its thoughtless calligraphy in the meadow. But it was more than wind that made the grass sway.

"Oh shit!" Gillian said.

I followed her gaze.

In the light of day, the eyes did not present as yellow. I imagine that effect was a nocturnal adaptation. As the grass danced their faces were revealed for just a moment. Almost human. Glimpsed and hidden. There and gone. Their eyes were pools of honey kissed by sunlight. They stared without blinking, almost human faces hidden within tufts of fur, gray and white like tree bark.

"They're everywhere," I whispered.

I had survival gear in my backpack but no weapons that would not have to be repurposed from their intended use. And I had no time. There were too many, and they were too close. If the attack happened, I would be overwhelmed before I took my backpack off. My head filled with the thunder of my own beating heart.

"What do we do?" Gillian asked, crouching, two arms wrapped around either our son or the idea of him.

There was nothing we could do. We were not in control of the moment. I showed my palms and averted my gaze. It was different than the wooly hippo, which was strange and wonderful. Dangerous, yes, but glimpsed from afar. They shifted back and forth, their faces blending so well with the tufted grass I lost track of them even at a distance of five feet. And unlike last night, they were silent.

Almost human. An earlier version, perhaps, a left turn on the evolutionary map. One leaned on a spear, his chin resting on his forearm. Quiet. Watching. The spear pointed to the sky, not me. Waiting. For what?

Thrown from the grass, the bandana sailed on the wind like a feather, landing at my feet. It was gritty with dried sweat.

"Oscar..."

The knife came next. It sank into the earth in front of my boots. The blade was brown with gummy blood.

Tears welled. He died alone, in the dark. A million miles from his little girl, who would only ever know her father through pictures. He had become a ghost. Like his dad. Like mine.

*Beyoop*

Muttered, stated as an afterthought. It echoed around us hardly louder than a whisper. Like fog, they weaved through the grass. Returning to their treetop perches, their lookouts. It was over. Whatever it had been.

"Oscar..."

***

Like the ocean turning shallow as it reached for the shore, the tall grass dwindled to stiff, blunted tufts. Half a mile beyond the great grass sea we found the site of his death. There was nothing left of him but blood on the ground. I was thankful for that. His name repeated in my head like a second heartbeat.

I had no sheath for the knife, so I held it. Every few seconds looking at the residue of Oscar's blood on the blade. I wanted to wipe it off, but I didn't. The blood meant he had lived and wiping it off would be the first step to forgetting him.

"I'm so sorry, Joe," Gillian said, her hand tentative on my shoulder.

Of course, this wasn't her fault, and it was an expected sentiment to be offered. My guttural response was unfocused, unwarranted anger that I did not express.

"Should I say something?" I asked, wondering how he contained all that blood inside of him, wondering where he was then.

"Say what you feel."

My relationship with Oscar was never easy to define. At the foundation of it was love. But not the easy kind of love I imagined two brothers shared. The love for our mother overlapped each other. Between us was that undeniable chunk of missing DNA. There were the obvious physical differences but the wedge between us was more subtle. Each of us, I think, waiting for that final betrayal, one our fathers levied upon us as children. One that would inevitably repeat itself. And so instead of growing close we circled each other like wolves from different packs, injured prey between us.

"I love you, Oscar," I began, and that was true. I always loved him. I just forgot how to show it. "Sorry it ended this way. I'm sorry you might have died questioning me. I love you, Oscar. You deserved to know it in life. I'll do everything I can to look after them. To let her know you were a good man."

\*\*\*

It was not far past the site of his death things began to change. I felt it on the nape of my neck, the hairs there scrunching, preparing me for...something. Gillian's body stiffened next to mind. She sensed it, too.

"Is it the Heart?" she asked.

"I hope not."

The change to the environment came next. The trees with glossy green leaves replaced by explosions of granite like bone jutting from an open fracture. Above, the sky was the color of chicken broth, clouds like tumors bubbling with instability. I had seen one like it after a tornado in Texas. I recognized the shift, but my thoughts were a mile behind. How many had it taken to kill him? Was he leading them away from us?

There was pressure in my ears. The weight of silence. My pulse quickened, the injured ankle throbbing as if another heart beat there. When had I last eaten? My water bottle was empty, and I had not seen a stream since yesterday afternoon.

"What day is it?" I asked Gillian, realizing I had forgotten to keep track as Pilot Bob advised.

Her body was taut against mine, fingernails needling my flesh. She pointed ahead and to the right. At that distance the fine details of its anatomy were lost. I squinted, my brain straining to fill the gaps of what it did not understand. It resembled a brown bear in shape, larger than I would have thought possible, but I had never seen one in person. It stood between two granite ribs, a still, smaller animal beneath it.

"It's...head," Gillian whispered.

Where the head should have been there were glistening petals of flesh, red and slick. Like the tentacles of a squid, the flesh petals collapsed and opened, billowed and drooped. As if tasting the air.

"It's feeding," I said.

"How? It doesn't-"

The petals went rigid, flinging blood and gore, and from the darkened center of the beast came two thin, black pincers. They prodded the kill, searched its form, pierced and parted the flesh. Then they retracted back into the creature, and an elephant-like trunk emerged. It was pink as a newborn mouse, but slick, obviously an organ typically housed within the body.

"Oh God, it's...it's guzzling the innards," Gillian said.

Fist-sized lumps tracked up the length of the trunk, as if it were swallowing apples whole.

"Do you think it can see us?" I whispered. We were not to the Heart yet but would have to pass in front of this thing to get there.

"How? It doesn't have eyes."

"Don't bears have a great sense of smell?"

"That's not a bear. Not anymore."

Hot breath tickled my ear. I lived ten lives in the space of a blink. We had not heard the approach, did not sense the surveillance.

"Run!" I said.

We did. In the brief moments my feet contacted earth I felt the thrum of our pursuer. Its breath was an acrid cloud around my face, copper and rot. Gillian pulled me like an attack dog at the end of its leash. Every step ignited a thousand new fractures in my ankle. The commotion of our sudden, loud exodus registered with the feeding thing. The trunk disappeared within the darkened center and the pincers emerged. I saw this with the stark, crystalline clarity of panic and through a lens of time that had been magnified, warped.

Sometimes, a stretch of barren road felt so much like Afghanistan my body reacted as if I'd been transported back. Lost in the shadow of the Hindu Kush, piloting a light truck whose gas gauge had been showing E for fifty miles. A decade later here I was again, in a starving land full of teeth.

"Fuck!"

The pincer punctured the slope of my shoulder like a cold sickle. I still had not seen it, our pursuer, but the pincer glimpsed peripherally suggested it was at least a cousin to the creature now on our right, abandoning carrion in search of fresher prey. The left half of my torso numbed, my arm flopping loosely against my side.

This is where we would die. Maybe this is how they died, the explorers and fortune seekers who came before us. For every headless man there were half a dozen who simply disappeared. Was there another Sam for them? A stranger who appeared at just the right time, when fear and desperation was at its peak, and showed them another path?

"Down!" Gillian screamed. I might have listened to her, or my body could have given out at the same instant. Something sailed over my head.

*Fsshhhhh*

"Keep running!" she screamed, jerking my useless arm, her attention diverted to the right.

The bear, what used to be a bear, stood on its hind legs. The flesh petals spread, a daisy yearning for sun. Like a snake shedding its skin, the creature slithered free, exiting through the darkened center of the exploded head. Black as the shadow of cemetery gates, there was no ready comparison to another animal. Nothing looked like this. I could only imagine its preferred environment, a cool hollow, its antennae tasting the tremors above. The bear carcass, then, was its manner of navigating a different environment.

"Just keep running!" Gillian huffed. Her backpack flew off her shoulders in the direction of the alien hunter. More stumbling forward than running, I obeyed, passing into the hazy shadow of a small mountain, hardly more than a hill, with a rocky outcrop bulging over the scorched earth like a defiant chin.

Rocks skidded underfoot. I fell, my cheek smacking gravel. In my confusion it seemed the earth reached up to strike me, the impact rattling my teeth like shaking a cup of ice. Pressure on my back. This was it. I'd been caught. In a moment, the pressure would grow cold, the pincer or proboscis knifing through the skin to skewer the organs beneath. I hoped it would be a quick end and that Gillian kept running when I fell.

"Joe," Gillian whispered in my ear. She shook me, the pressure on my back moving to my shoulder. It was her hand. "They stopped following us."

She brushed my cheek, popped gravel free from the skin. I saw her clearly through one eye. The other was foggy from the collision. She hoisted me into a sitting position. Though dazed I saw it was true. The bear-thing that lanced my shoulder shook the loose tendrils of its ruined face. They were orange from the can of bear spray Gillian had thrown. The other hunter stood at the edge of the shadow cast by our mountain.

"I think it's afraid," she said. "Or maybe it knows something we don't."

I touched my cheek, pockmarks leaking blood.

Gillian winced, "Just grow a beard and you'll be good as new. How's the arm?"

I almost said *fine* because I felt no pain there. But I failed at lifting it, managing only to twitch my shoulder.

"I hope it's not permanent," I said, then looked past her to the outcrop. "I think we're here."

She scooted behind and poked her head between my arm and ribs.

"One, two, three," she said. We stood, nearly tumbled, then hobbled up the gravel path. Slipping and sliding, but never falling, we left avalanches in our wake. The border of the outcrop was lined with jagged rocks like natural tombstones. The remnants of a wall?

The black hunter had reentered the bear hide, the flesh petals collapsing around the corpse beneath it. The creature hauled its prize away to feed alone. Once it disappeared there was nothing else to see.

"I guess this is it," I said.

***

There were gaps in the ceiling of the cave, shafts of sickly light like unwashed curtains. She held my good hand as we shuffled forward, the fear of what was behind as powerful as what might lie ahead. We did not know what we were looking for. We knew the Heart was near but could not qualify that distance. We might have to descend into darkness for miles.

The gravity of the Heart was undeniable. Like fish on a hook, it pulled us forward. We groped blindly, the light from the mouth fading to nothing. The floor angled down, giving momentum to my uncoordinated steps.

Forward, in darkness. Like satellites succumbing to the will of the larger planet. This was inevitable.

This was the end.

The Heart, as it presented to me, was a vertical, oily pool. An upright pond stretching from the cave floor to its ceiling, with no gaps along the wall. This was it. There was no way past it. A wall of rippling black, like the night was stolen from the sky. Starlight tipped the turbulent waves.

"Joseph," Gillian whispered.

"Yes?" I said, unable to face her.

She guided my hand, pressed my palm against her belly. I didn't understand why, but then I remembered. Beneath my palm the shirt was loose, the fabric no longer stressed by a growing life.

"Oh Joe," she sobbed.

"Gillian..."

She separated from me, the pinpricks of starlight spotlighting her in glimpses. It felt like before, the delivery room after the nurses left. I had no words for her then, nothing to blunt the pain, to take some of it from her. Her cheeks sparkled with tears as she reached inside the pocket of her jeans and withdrew...a bundle of sticks, tightly wrapped with twine.

"What?"

"The baby monitor," she said, and dropped it on the cave floor, where it broke apart. "Was any of it real?"

I would have asked her the same thing if I thought she had the answer.

"I'm sorry," I said, hugging her with my good arm.

She cried into my chest, softly, as she had at night twenty years ago, when she feared waking me. In twenty years, I still had not found the right words because there were none. And so I did not speak. I held her as I should have before.

Minutes passed before her static hands began to rub my back, her shaking breaths steadying to a stream passed through pursed lips.

"I'm okay," she said. "Okay enough."

Sam did not reveal how the Heart functioned. Recalling him revived the questions he proposed, the assertions about his origins.

"Chaos engine," I muttered.

"What?" she sputtered.

"A chaos engine. That's what Sam called it. It introduces chance."

My fingers hovered an inch from the crest of the tallest waves. What if I touched it? What if I pulled one of those stars free from the abyss?

"Don't," Gillian said, lowering my arm.

"I wasn't I-"

Sniffling, she picked up the scattered sticks, wrapped the twine around them and tied it off. She nodded as she did this, a decision made then, or confirmed.

"Let me go first."

"Go?!" I nearly shouted.

"Neither of us knows what's happening here. Any explanation is a guess. But there are some things I feel, stronger than knowing if that makes sense."

It did, in a way, but I extended no lifeline.

"I haven't been talking to myself, Joe," she said.

Starlight glinted in her eyes, her gaze as hard as stones.

"I didn't-" I began, but she put a hand up to stop me.

"I've been talking with him for twenty years. Since he was a bump in my belly, a thought before that. And I know it wasn't the same for you. Part of me hurt, but another part of me understood. We needed different things from this life. I have my guesses but only you know for sure. What I needed from this life was not to be a mother. It was to be *his* mother. Only him. That's why I couldn't let go. Why I couldn't forget."

"I still don't understand what that has to do with this...whatever it is."

"Like I said, we're both guessing. But I don't think it works any other way. I don't think you and I leave this place hand-in-hand, walk peacefully back to the campsite and go home with Pilot Bob. Start a new life together. That's not why we're here, Joe. And you've got your own decision to make, but I've made mine. My only request is that you let me go first."

*Let me go.*

I held her hands tighter as she said the words. For so long, Gillian's love was the foundation upon which I built everything else. The confidence to lead men, to ask another woman to marry me, came from the perfect love she had shown me. To let her go meant I was losing that forever.

As if she heard the thought, she said, "I hope I filled you up so that you can go on living without me."

It was then she relinquished my fingers and took a step back. She placed the bundle of sticks on the floor, carefully, looked at her hand and smiled, then showed me the splinters in her fingertips.

Gillian was always supposed to be there, but in that moment what choice did I have? What influence did I have? Yes, she loved me. Had always loved me. But it wasn't my love she had conversations with in the stillness of the night, when only the crickets were listening.

I hugged her, felt the fluttering in my chest settle, our heartbeats a mirror. Letting go of Gillian felt like cutting off a part of me and casting it into the deepest part of the ocean. She pulled away first because I did not have the will to, then she took my hands. I felt the pressure of her fingers in my left, but not the texture of them.

"It's always been you, Joe. I knew it the first day. I think I also knew you would never feel the same. Maybe you're a little closer now, at the end. Isn't it funny how that works? If we're just guessing about what happens next, I'm going to have to take that chance."

*Chance*

"What are you hoping for?"

She smiled and framed a belly that was no longer there.

"I hope it's you, and me, and him. Another lifetime. Another possibility. I'm not sad, Joe. I could go on living this life. But I know that would be my last thought on this earth. So why wait fifty more years? Now, do me one last favor."

I nodded.

"Close your eyes."

\*\*\*

There was no sound after the shuffle of her feet and a final, deep breath. I opened my eyes to find I was alone. The vertical pool of oil and stars rippled where she entered, the last evidence of her other than the sticks on the cave floor. The waves persisted, growing taller, more violent. I stepped back and to the side as the darkness parted and something, some flying thing, emerged.

It could have been made of glass, hints of structure only revealed in flashes by the silver-tipped waves. There was no obvious mechanism for flight, no wings or source of propulsion. I thought of a jellyfish in water. Its movements were similar, a gentle rise and fall, though I felt no breeze. It swam through the air, disappearing. I followed its likely path considering the pace it established and caught sight of it again as it entered the milky shaft of light. There it exploded in color and fell to the ground, shattering.

*Chance*

Is that how it worked? An exchange between worlds? Between realities? Had the monsters in bear costumes come through here? Or had they always been?

Gillian was gone. Oscar was dead. Mom was dead. And my dad...

I did not know if the Heart was the answer for me, because I did not understand the question. Would I simply step into another world, one potentially inhospitable to my anatomy? Would I wake up in the delivery room to find Gillian rubbing her belly, winking at me as if to say *I told you so.*

My fingers danced above the waves, a whisper away from those possibilities. Everything I loved was behind me. There was no guarantee it would be better. My fingers danced and I scraped my soul searching for the question.

I did not feel the impact, but the next thing I knew I was dreaming.

# CHAPTER NINE

I woke in iterations, pain announcing itself in my ankle and shoulder. A duller pain rumbled below my right ear. That was new. I reached for it and found my hands were bound, the right arm supporting the weight of the left.

"You were gonna go in," Oscar said.

He sat opposite me, back against the cave wall, the shaft of light between us.

"Sorry for the blow, but I thought if you heard me it might startle you enough to make you touch it accidentally. Also, I had to buy myself a little time," he said, then lifted his hands, miming my bound wrists. "And thanks for the knife. Thought I lost that."

"Oscar I...I thought you were dead."

"I'll get to that, but I have to get something off of my chest first."

I couldn't see him well, was not sure if this was even real. The remnants of the flying thing sparkled on the cave floor. In the low light of the cave and in my groggy state he could have been anyone.

"I've wanted to kill you since we were boys."

The statement sat between us like an unexploded bomb. It sounded like a line rehearsed a thousand times, disconnected from the passion of its initial tellings.

"Of all the things I've been sure about in life, I was most sure that I wanted to kill you. I wanted to kill you when you came back from your dad's with a new Chicago Bulls jersey. I wanted to kill you when you ran crying to Mom because he didn't show up. I wanted to kill you when you watched TV, not studying, not worried about homework because you could just do it on the bus. And you would. And what you wrote in five minutes would be better than what I could write in five years. It was always so easy for you."

He exhaled and twiddled his thumbs. The broken creature was between us like a shattered whiskey glass.

"My dad hated me. Comparing myself to you, how could I expect anything different from Mom? So, I did what I had to. I made myself feel better. Quieted the questions."

He sat up, dusted off his hands and bent his knees so that his chin rested atop them.

"Do you know how easy it was to blame it on you?"

I shook my head.

"Nothing has ever been easy for me. But it's been getting there, lately. Not easy but not as painful. I've got a good life, Bro. There's a kid at home that's got me wrapped around her little finger. A woman I've loved for ten years. Can you believe that? Ten years?

"I've been clean longer than I ever wasn't. And still, I carried that anger with me. Through childhood. Through all the bullshit. So, that's why I wrote that letter. The one that's probably in your pocket right now. I found the others when I helped Mom rearrange the office a couple years ago. And I knew about this place. Just some Internet journey I took years ago. I thought about it every now and then. Somehow, the ideas came together, my hatred for you and my wonder about Nahanni.

"But how to get you up here? All I had to do was sign that letter from him. I knew you would go. Just had to wait Mom out."

As he spoke, I shifted my hands, creating space. The knot wasn't tight.

"I can see you, and you don't have to worry about it. If I was going to kill you, I could've done it after I knocked you out.

"So, what was the plan? Why didn't I just kill you in your own home? Maybe because I didn't really want to. Maybe that's why I added all these extra steps. Fly to this...place. Every step was an opportunity to back out, but I didn't. I bought the tickets and the gear, wasn't even thinking about killing you when I did it. But this conversation? That's part of the plan. I was going to sit across from you at the top of the world, where only you could hear me, and tell you I hated you. And I might have done the other part, but this place had another destiny for me.

"I didn't plan for Gillian, but that was okay. I only needed you alone for an hour, an accidental death, up here, isn't tough to pull off. Now that I think about it, it's this conversation I wanted. Not the killing. I've hated you since I understood what that word meant. Hate."

I dropped my hands in my lap, no longer fighting the restraints. We were middle-aged men. The stakes were higher, but the dance was the same. Between us was not just a broken creature. Between us were the shadows of two men we never understood, whose influence filled our sails in silence.

He continued, "I loved you before. Somewhere my love for you got twisted. Once the momentum started building in that direction, I couldn't get control. Until now. I've told myself I hated you. It's understandable considering our childhoods. Considering the gifts we were or weren't given. But it's not true. It's the biggest lie I've ever told. And I told it to my damn self. Year after year after year.

"I never hated you, Bro. I hated what I thought you saw when you looked at me. I hated my own reflection. So, this is how it's gonna work. I'm gonna go back to get help, from Pilot Bob or whoever. The ranger station if need be. I'm not strong enough to carry you, and if you try to walk we'll both die. The rope is to buy me time, because I know if I didn't do it you would come after me. You would try to stop me."

Oscar the child, full of hate. Reinforced by a monster. And what did I do? It was *his* problem, just like Gillian's grief was hers. I had questions about everything he shared, but the shock of seeing him, alive, pushed them to the back of my mind.

"How did you make it? We saw...the creatures in the trees. All that blood?"

"Oh, that wasn't my blood. That was something else I don't have words for. Wasn't a problem for them, though. Yellow eyes. Took it down like, like that old outside cat we used to have. Remember the one who left baby birds on our doorstep? Took it down just like that."

"They helped you?"

He shrugged, "Maybe we helped each other. You have what's left of my water and most of the food. I'm traveling light. Don't know how long it's gonna take, and this cave is probably the safest place for you right now. But Joseph, don't go inside. You have a niece who is going to love you. She already does."

He left before I could make a promise I did not intend to keep.

\*\*\*

My legs were also bound. Though the knots were tight the material was weak. Twenty minutes after Oscar left, I hobbled to the mouth of the cave. I could not see him, only the tipped stone obelisks protruding from the earth.

Recognition came suddenly, like stepping back from a connect-the-dots picture. The pieces were there, broken by time. The stones along the outcrop were not remnants of a wall. The holes in the cave ceiling not the effect of millennia of rain battering a weak spot.

It was a skull. I stood in its open mouth. Before me was what was left of the body, bones hardened to stone, seized and shifted by nature.

It was a skull. Perhaps *heart* was the wrong word for the anatomy that persisted beyond its death. Giant was too small a word. Maybe god was better.

"I'm sorry, Oscar," I said, then reentered the cave.

# CHAPTER TEN

In the cabin, time lost meaning but still felt linear. Still went forward despite the absence of typical landmarks to indicate its progression. In the Heart, time did not make sense. I had been tossed into a cosmic rock tumbler. That was more a sensation of undoing than anything physical. I lost contact with my body, with what I identified as *me*. With those components stripped away there was only the base. The original component upon which all others would be layered.

I assume I was in darkness because the alternative is an image I cannot conjure. I had thoughts and memories stretched across time. I had memories of moments I had not experienced, memories of moments that *had* happened but in a different way. I had access to every possible moment and every lived moment. I sensed beyond that immediate understanding, beyond the confines of Joseph there were still more possibilities. Other lives and times stretching back to the base of the Universe, the building blocks that would become everything. I sensed Gillian and the life inside of her like a small, hot sun. There were versions of us who raised him together, an infinite number of them. There were versions of us who persisted after the stillbirth. I wanted to stay with her. To understand more. But I was in the tumbler and did not have control.

There was Sam, a kite in an updraft, sailing past me in the space between heartbeats. Oscar, a million million possibilities of him.

Mom.

Outside of time.

I was not reduced but revealed.

The mind and the brain were not the same. One persisted in this space while the other was tied to a body. The body an aperture.

Tumbling. Tumbling. I might have fallen forever, through the framework of the Universe into what lay beneath. Instead, I landed.

\*\*\*

It was not waking from a dream, not death. A space between death and life. From nothingness. I was first aware of the breath in my lungs, the automatic functions my body performed. My heart beating in my chest, sweat forming on my brow. It was dark there. Dark in a way that felt connected to reality as I understood it.

There was soil beneath my fingers as warm as the air around me. There were no additional inputs. No sound. No breeze across my skin. My memories were like a shuffled deck of cards. One I glimpsed was similar to what I experienced then. I stood, unafraid of contacting the ceiling, because I knew it would not be there. I began to walk. No other option presented itself.

I had done this before. This exact ritual. An idea began to form. I was in the cabin. Maybe I had never left.

I walked because I had to. I walked and as my thoughts settled, two emerged from the deck. Where was Gillian and my son? Where was Oscar? If I was still in the cabin, they might be alive. Though my relationship to that concept, alive, had shifted. Life was a modality, an opportunity for the Universe to make peace with itself.

As if the reorganization of my thoughts was the catalyst, the light, faint from distance but bright in the absence of all other light, gave purpose to my wandering.

Would I see something different this time? I rested my chin on the windowsill, inserted my fingers between the blinds and parted them. It was evening outside unlike last time. The driveway was empty. I had not expected a different result, and I worried the *lesson* I was supposed to have learned did not grow sufficiently deep roots.

To the right, above the wicker chairs, there was a light. It came through the kitchen but originated in the dining room. I walked through the room from my childhood into a hallway with gaps between its pictures. Fathers recently dispatched to a box in the closet.

There was the L-shaped couch in the living room, space to grow for a family that only dwindled. The television housed within one hundred pounds of wood was frozen. Maybe Oscar was somewhere in the house with the remote tucked in his underwear. There was the plastic tree, the leaves of which somehow fell as if it was real. Oscar was forced to dust it because Mom didn't allow me to use the spray. I smiled, realizing he was probably responsible for the missing leaves.

This kitchen was not a place to make memories. There was no love in its design, just cupboards and countertops, an oven and dishwasher slightly different shades of white.

I turned the corner into the dining room.

"Mom?"

She, this version of her, was probably in her mid-forties, the gray at her temples growing out faster than her enthusiasm to dye it.

"Hello Joseph."

"Where are we? Mom I- I've missed you."

She gestured to the chair across from her. I sat and she took my hands in hers.

"I'm just beginning to remember. Where we come from. Why we're here at all."

"Y- you were there. You were there when I was falling."

She squeezed my hands, "You sensed your connection to me, dear. We have always been connected."

"It felt real. It felt more real than anything."

"This space between us is the illusion, Joseph. There is no distance, no difference. You can feel it sometimes. I did. At night when I thought of you and Oscar, and it felt like there were three hearts in my chest. When you left to start your life, to explore the world, we didn't separate. My soul thinned and stretched to accommodate."

She rubbed her thumbs over my knuckles.

"I do miss the way this feels."

"Mom, why am I here? Did you...did you bring me here?"

She winked, "You were falling. I just gave you a nudge. Why do you think you're here?"

I could not define the word, *here*, to respond meaningfully.

"I don't know. I thought I came to the park, to Nahanni to reconnect with Oscar. That idea seems so small now."

"You never know the why while you're in it. What would be the point of living? You aren't in it now, son. So why are you here?"

I freed my hand to search my pockets. There was no letter. Had I taken it with me?

"The letters. Mom, why didn't you give them to me?"

"I did, Joseph. I gave them to you at first. You read them and your dad never followed through on his promises. You would wait for him at that window. I came home from work one day and found sweat spots from your chin all the way down the windowsill. You were there for hours, walking back and forth, your poor little chin leaving sweat spots behind. I even gave them to you after that. Eventually, your anger grew bigger than your hope."

"I...read them?"

"Some. Some you threw away without opening."

"Why don't I remember?"

Mom looked out the window. Shadows from the fence across the small concrete slab that served as our patio. There were a few potted plants there, her first, timid attempt at gardening. A ghost of a smile rippled. I wondered what she was thinking about.

"You tucked him away in a closet, but you didn't close the door. I imagine you walked past it every day. Some part of you knew what was in there, what you would find if you opened the door.

"And you might wonder, knowing what you know now, why you would have chosen this pain. I can't answer that question for you, but I can tell you what I discovered for myself. Sometimes it's the pain that gets you out of bed in the morning. Sometimes it's the pain, not love that makes you question your place in the Universe. You chose the pain to discover something about yourself."

Mom scooted her chair backwards and stood.

"I remember this house. It was too big and too small at the same time. I was afraid it wasn't enough for you and Oscar. I was afraid I failed you because you wore hand-me-down clothes, and Oscar's were bought from the thrift store to begin with," she said, smiling at the oven where Christmas cookies were baked and burnt in equal measure. "Funny how none of that matters now. And did it really matter then?"

We walked together, past the plastic tree with its missing leaves, the couch big enough for Oscar and me to nap on at the same time. We walked to the front door. Mom stood on tiptoe to hug me. We stayed that way for a long time. She pulled away first and in her hand she held an envelope.

"I don't know the question you asked, what you hope to discover about yourself. But here is an answer anyway."

I took the envelope from her. She curled my fingers around it.

"Mom," I said with sudden urgency. "Is Gillian where you are? My son?"

*Dad?*

"The space between us is an illusion, Joseph. Now, you have to let me go."

She opened the door, not waiting for a response.

"I miss this neighborhood. There were pecan trees just over there," she said, pointing. "Remember how you and Oscar would fill up your bags and try to sell them to the neighbors?"

I did remember, but I did not have time to tell her. The door closed and the world went black.

\*\*\*

Light leaked through the slats. The steady drone of rushing water. Whistling, a song I did not recognize.

As if running from a live grenade, I dove through the hide door and into the light of day. Sweet air in my lungs, grass beneath my fingers. Through my eyelids the world was electric blue. I blinked, taking tiny sips of light.

"Pilot Bob said you wouldn't come back."

Oscar sat with his back against the shack, an open can of beans between his legs.

"After the first week I thought he was right."

"First...week?"

"After the second week I was almost sure of it, but I couldn't leave."

"How long has it been? How did you know I would be here?"

He sat up, scratched the scruff of his mostly silver beard.

"Because we're brothers."

\*\*\*

Bob wouldn't be back for a few days, which meant Oscar and I had the park to ourselves, like he had wanted. He told me about the journey back to the original campsite, how hours of walking returned him to the Heart. Over and over again.

"I almost went through it when I didn't find you there. I thought it would be better than dying alone."

"What changed?"

He shrugged and scratched his beard again.

"I don't know. I tried to picture you in front of me, like I was following you. I might have been delirious, but it felt like you were really there," he said, then stopped and unzipped his backpack. "I found this. Think it's for you."

I took the baby monitor from him.

"I turned it on. It works. Uh, like I said, though, it's for you."

I told him about Mom, about what I thought happened traveling through the Heart.

"What did it say?" he asked.

"It?"

"You said she gave you an envelope."

I retrieved it from my pocket, unfolded it and broke the seal. Her writing was wispy, barely a ghost on the page.

*You have always been enough.*

The End

# AFTERWORD

There is a seed of truth at the center of this story. My brother, Jimmie, and I are half-brothers, though we have never thought of each other in these terms. We do have different fathers, but his was simply absent, not abusive like Oscar's father.

Jimmie is dyslexic. He is brilliant in many ways I could never be, but often not in the way that seemingly mattered in school. He understands space and shapes in a way my mind can't comprehend. I understand language in the same way he understands space and shapes. The differences between us were apparent to me as a child. The hate Oscar carried in this story is actually the fear I felt from a young age.

How could Jimmie not hate me? How could he not be bitter that his gifts were not valued in the same way as mine?

I think I would be. I fear I would be.

When given the opportunity to speak at my big brother's wedding, I told him he was my hero. I don't think I ever told him that before. I should have.

He taught me how to ride a bike. He protected me and my sister (singular because you weren't born yet, Kelsea) from spiders. He used one of his first paychecks to buy me a pair of Jordans, which I wore until they fell apart.

I love you, big brother.

There is truth with Gillian's character too, wondering what my life would look like if I had walked a different path. By the way Joseph's character is written, the path is lonelier than the one I chose.

I first read about Nahanni National Park a decade or so ago. The lore about the headless men is not very deep, but it is consistent. Although I could have leaned into the potential violence of headless men, it was the other tales that interested me. Giants, mammoths, and the entrance to the inner earth...

There is a short story version of this novella in my second collection, *The Rat King*. There is a novel version of this story collecting digital dust in an agent's inbox from a #pitdark event two years ago. I've been fascinated by the Valley, but I needed the right characters. Looking inward rather than creating characters from nothing changed everything. I think I got it right this time.

# ACKNOWLEDGMENTS

Dana from Nahanni River Adventures kindly answered many questions about the park, the conditions one would find at specific times of the year, including the detail that the rivers would be cloudy with debris, which was something I had gotten wrong in previous iterations of this story. Thank you, Dana, for answering a random email from a guy in Texas!

My good friend, Brett Bullion, created the art for the cover. Brett has given life to more than a dozen of my stories now, and he nails the vision every time.

My other good friend, Geoff, took an idea and helped it become the amazing cover to this book. Was a pleasure working with you, and I hope this is the first of many covers to come!

Joe at Cemetery Gates is one of the best people in horror. And he also has great taste in music.

A special thank you to the Texas Horror Crew: Max and Lori Booth, Celso Hurtado, Agatha Andrews, Grace Reynolds, Johnny Compton, R.J. Joseph, and Ryan Bradley. (This list could be much longer, but these are the friends who paid me to mention them). Grace and Celso both read a draft version of this story and provided outstanding feedback. Thank you again!

Thank you to the readers, reviewers, bookstores, and libraries.

**L.P. Hernandez** is an author of horror and speculative fiction. His stories have been featured in anthologies from Cemetery Dance, Dark Matter Ink, and the Howl Society among others. He is a regular contributor to *The NoSleep Podcast* and has released two short story collections. His third collection titled *No Gods, Only Chaos* will be published by Cemetery Dance in 2024. His novella, *Stargazers*, kicked off the My Dark Library line of novellas curated by Sadie "Mother Horror" Hartmann and published through Cemetery Gates Media. L.P. also hosts *Dog-eared Nightmares*, a podcast about well-loved horror. When not writing, L.P. serves as a medical administrator in the U.S. Air Force. He is a husband, father, and a dedicated metalhead.

Printed in Great Britain
by Amazon